Ray Ruppert

THE VOICE OF CON

Tex Ware
Everett, WA

ISBN-13: 978-1-935500-48-3

THE VOICE OF CON

Acknowledgments:

To my wonderful wife, Terri. Thank you for believing in me, and for your work in editing.

To those who have gallantly served their country in the armed forces of the United States, as well as for others who have served in the fight for freedom.

To Jesus for all you have done; the Bible says it much better than I can. Thank you.

Chapter One

"This is a grave criminal act that has occurred in your branch," I snap at the old guy in an expensive suit. I poke him in the chest with my index finger and he backs up to the window looking out high over Seattle and Puget Sound. It's a perfect day with the sun shining and not a cloud in the sky, but rain is splattering on the window, obscuring the view.

"I wouldn't keep my client's assets here even if the president of the company assured me they would be safe. So, unless you want me to call the FBI, you will immediately prepare me bearer certificates for all of his stocks and bonds. In addition, you will provide a cashier's check for all the cash in the account and we'll wait right here while you do that. In addition, I will be taking this documentation with me." I pick up a stack of papers from the desk.

The old man starts to protest, then suddenly leaves in a huff.

"Wow, Darryl, you're getting quite assertive," says Renee.

"I think we're in danger. We need to get those certificates and clear out as quickly as possible. Keep an eye on the door," I say as I look out at the snow. That doesn't look right. I turn and make a phone call but can't hear myself. The phone must not be working right.

The old guy soon returns with a briefcase. I go over the bearer certificates to make sure they match everything on the account documents from the desk. Next, I'm quickly moving through a maze of cubicles and exit to a lobby. Where did Renee go?

Renee is right there with me as we get on an elevator and I push a button. The elevator plunges down. My stomach feels like it's going in the opposite direction. We stop suddenly and I get out. I go around the corner to another elevator lobby. I look for Renee but she's gone again. A door opens and I get on another elevator. Renee is already on the elevator and we continue down.

"Where did you go?" I ask.

"Huh?" she answers and starts taking off her clothes.

I start to watch, but the elevator door opens and we get out. This is getting too weird. I'm starting to think this is a dream, but if it were, then we would still be in the elevator and – instead we are running down the stairs and Renee is fully dressed, in a suit no less.

At the door to the lobby I motion to Renee to be quiet as I slowly open the door a crack and look into the elevator lobby. I let the door close after my peek.

"It's all clear. No one is waiting for us. Let's make a break for it before someone shows up." I say.

I look out the door again and whisper, "Come on." We walk slowly into the lobby and look around the corner. As we exit through the revolving door and head up the street, I look back and see two menacing guys following us. We hurry up the street in the bright sunshine and weave in and around people walking on the sidewalk with their umbrellas up. Why does everyone have an umbrella? I mean everyone has one; there isn't a single person without one and the sun is shining, not a cloud in the sky. We quickly get in our old VW bug and I start the car.

I see a bright flash of light and I sit up suddenly. Oh crap, I fell asleep on the couch. I see Renee standing in front of the window with bright sunlight shining from the only crack in the clouds through our apartment window.

"Hey, Darryl, why were all the blinds closed?" asks Renee. "Were you meditating and fell asleep again?"

"Yeah," I admit sheepishly. This meditating stuff that Joe wants me to learn just isn't my style.

"Well, I hope you're prepared for tonight, meditation or not," continues Renee as she sets a small bag of groceries on the table. "This took just about all of our last five bucks."

I think back about my dream. I was meditating before everything went weird. The Voice had told me to pay attention. Maybe it wasn't a dream; maybe I was being shown the future. But what was the bright light? No, it was just Renee opening the blinds. However, I could certainly use a briefcase of bearer certificates; wow, what I couldn't do with that!

After dinner, we walk the six blocks to where we left my car. It's drizzling and I'm not in all that great of a mood. Renee isn't talking much either.

We get in and drive south and east until we get on N.E. Pacific Street and drive past the University of Washington Medical Center. The hospital plays an important part in our plans to make some money tonight. We continue right and cross the Montlake Drawbridge and on up to Capitol Hill.

Renee and I slow down and try to get a better look at the Capitol Hill mansion. The windows on the 1952 VW bug are fogged, making it even harder to see through the dark night and rain. There are no parking places on the narrow street so we circle another block and find one.

"Well, I hope this turns out to be a better party than the last one," grumbles Renee. "We're going to be soaked by the time we walk back."

"Yeah, me too, if we don't find a mark soon, we'll have to go to work to pay the rent," I reply. "Let's try not to forget our umbrella this time," I say as we get out of the car.

"My source said that this party is being thrown by some rich kid by the name of Rodney. He's a nerd dropout because he's been partying too much. All his friends are mostly engineering and science students. If they are as nerdy as I hope, we should be able to find someone gullible enough to 'help us out.'" I laugh aloud at that.

So far, Renee and I have been able to make a fairly decent living conning students around the University of Washington. We've used various schemes and even some outright begging. We have a one-room apartment on the Ave that only costs $85 a month, a bit of furniture, and a killer stereo system. Being on the fringe of the hippy lifestyle has its advantages, as we don't need much, other than food and weed.

Tonight may be a breaker, though, as rent is due in just three days, Monday to be exact, and our luck has been terrible. At our last party we almost got caught stooping to rifling through purses in our desperation. That's not something we like to do as it's too easy to get caught and even arrested. So far, our record is clean.

After I get out of the car, I grab the umbrella from behind my seat where Renee tossed it and rush around to hold it over her but she doesn't wait for me to open the door. I don't lock it, even in this neighborhood. No one wants to steal that junker or even break in.

"I'm going to get water spots on my jumper," complains Renee.

I like her outfit but wonder if it's right for tonight. She looks like herself but I would have thought she would dress up more for an engineering party. Oh, well, ankle-length-denim-jumpered, flower-bloused hippy is what I have as a sidekick tonight. She is a good one though, a good shill but just a so-so hippy. I dig the beige shawl and headband with straight hair, but I don't think the bleach blond quite goes with it but I'm not going to make a big deal about it. I'm not that dumb.

She catches me looking at her, "What are you looking at?"

"Are you sure the hippy look is right for tonight? You know, with all the nerds that will be there?" I question her, wishing I hadn't asked when she gives me a dirty look before she gets all smug looking, sticking her nose in the air.

"You'll see."

There is nothing but silence as we walk the next half block.

Renee breaks the silence, "By the way, Darryl, where did you learn to be a nerd? Do you really think engineering students wear light blue shirts with button down collar and gray slacks to parties? You might fit into a classroom. I hope your typical male engineering student isn't that square." She shakes her head. "If they look like you, this is going to be one boring party. Hey, did you remember your pocket protector?" she teased. "I should have brought a coat though, it's cold tonight."

"Well, it is April, it is Seattle, and it is raining. Why do you think I wore the trench coat?"

We climb up the ten steps to the gate, stop, and gawk at the huge two story old Victorian house. The upstairs has a balcony over the porch with a circular entry on the left. The gate is open so we continue up the walkway and the five steps onto the broad porch. The living room window reveals a large crowd of people who have already arrived. I shake out the umbrella and fold it up.

"Whoa, this is quite a house, Darryl. The living room is huge; there must be twenty or more people in there," exclaims Renee.

"This indeed may be our lucky night," I reply as we turn left, and use the doorknocker to bang on the front door.

We can hear music, laughing, and loud conversations through the door but no one answers. I bang again, harder. We wait but the noise of the party must keep anyone from hearing.

Renee looks at me with upraised eyebrows and a half smile she uses when asking an unspoken question.

I shrug my shoulders and open the door. The round entry way is a good six feet in diameter with polished hardwood floor and a round oriental rug in the middle. There are other umbrellas leaning on the wall, on the sitting bench beneath the windows, and laying on the floor. I follow suit and put mine down behind the door, ignoring the puddle of water from the other umbrellas.

A closet door is open at the end of the entryway but there isn't any room for my trench coat. I take off my coat and looked around. There's another sitting bench against the dark brown wooden staircase leading upstairs. Coats are piled on it several deep so I drop mine there.

"You want me to put your shawl here?" I ask Renee.

"No, it'll get all wet; besides, I need to warm up first."

She walks into the next room and stops in front of the huge fireplace, extending her hands toward the cheery blaze between two stone lions on the hearth.

So far, no one has said boo to us so I tell Renee that I'm going to find us a beer and head for the kitchen. It's crowded but I manage to elbow my way in and get a couple of Rainiers out of the refrigerator. It has to be the biggest refrigerator I've seen outside of a restaurant.

When I get back to the fireplace, I find that Renee has already made a contact. She's talking to another young lady who looks like she just got off the Ave, long brown hair with a headband, no less. An oversized green paisley blouse is draped over her plain brown ankle-length skirt. How did a hippy like her get the news of this nerdy party? I hand Renee her beer.

"Hi, Darryl, I'd like you to meet Jennifer. She's the president of Tau Beta Pi," smirks Renee.

"So?" I gesture with my free hand with an open circular motion.

Renee rolls her eyes and shakes her head back and forth.

Jennifer explains, "It's the engineering honor society. Where have you been?"

I grit my teeth. It's too early to be busted and tossed out. "So what's your major?" I ask, hoping to find a good comeback that she can't bust.

"Electrical engineering," she says.

Whew, I can go with that. "I'm pre-med so I don't pay too much attention to engineering things."

"Well, I guess I can excuse that," she answers with smile that I really don't know how to read. Is she coming on to me or just being nice? One glance at Renee and I know that I shouldn't try to find out.

"So where's our host? I went straight for the brew and didn't see him." Since I haven't ever met him, I need a clue and hope Jennifer doesn't catch on.

"Mr. Downer is over there on the couch." She points with her chin.

I turn around to see the back of a guy's head slouched on the couch ignoring all that is going on around him including the hot babe with the maxi-mini skirt standing almost in front of him. If I had his vantage point I wouldn't be staring at my navel.

"What's with him? Too much of a good thing?" I ask, not really expecting an answer.

"Got his draft call. He has to report for his physical on Monday. I can hardly blame him," replies Jennifer.

The Voice says to me that this guy will be fruitful.

"Maybe I can cheer him up." I abruptly leave the two ladies to finish their hippy chatting.

I make my way over to couch and walk around to see Rodney's face which corresponds to his slouch. Man, what a sad-sack. I check him over to make sure he fits a mark. Longish brown hair, bell-bottom tweed slacks (ugh) and a flowery shirt with the top two buttons open. Good enough.

There's still enough room to sit down beside him. I plop down to make sure he can't totally ignore me. He turns to give me a half smile then looks down at his hands again. The hot babe is now gyrating to "The Yellow Submarine" but Rodney still isn't interested. This might be hard to do especially if Rodney has been using.

"I heard the bad news, Rod." I have to break the ice somehow.

Rodney just grunts.

"So what's your plan? You going to Canada while you have a chance?"

"If I did that, I'd lose everything, so it's not an option. But if I go to 'Nam and get killed then it's no better." Rodney is coherent but still looking down and shaking his head.

I lean over to make sure he hears as I lower my voice, "I may have an option for you. I've helped others get out of it and able to get on with their lives here. You interested?" I hope I haven't been too quick leading in but something about Rodney's voice leads me to believe that The Voice is right and he will bite.

Now Rodney is staring straight into my face, eyes squinted slightly and eyebrows furrowed. "You serious? It has to be entirely foolproof."

I relax; this is going to work. I can see the rent cash already. Renee has moved around now into my line of sight. I glance at her but quickly focus on Rodney, looking straight into his eyes. I slowly nod so Renee knows the hook is in.

"Do you know John Scruggs?" I ask as I drop my chin so it looks like I'm talking to his chest but keeping my eyes on him.

Puzzled, Rodney replies, "The name sounds familiar, but I can't place him."

That's because he is a fictitious guy I made up. John is a familiar name and most people have heard of Earl Scruggs the bluegrass banjo player. Put the two together and my man thinks he just might know him.

"OK, John was one of my clients. He had just flunked out of engineering after only three quarters. He was engaged to a cute brunette and was scared spitless about getting drafted, which is exactly what happened." Now I look both ways as if to make sure no one is listening and lean a bit closer to Rodney.

"I was able to make sure he flunked his physical and didn't get called up."

Rodney's eyes get wide, "Really? H-how did you do that?"

Thank you, Lord, that he's already had a few beers but not too many. This seems almost too easy and I can't take a chance of being overconfident. I take a deep breath.

"We have a way to make it look like you're mentally impaired without it showing up on any drug tests." I pause to make sure it sinks in. "We provide documents that show this is a long term condition so you don't get called back in later for any other kind of follow up. And if you do, we'll be available to get you through that one too." That is, if we haven't already moved on.

"Hey man, at this point, I'm ready to do just about anything as long as I don't end up in jail. Have you ever been caught doing this?" Rod is looking really nervous, sweating now, and wringing his hands.

I stiffen up as if insulted. "Rodney, I'm here talking to you. If I had ever been caught, do you think I'd be free right now? Let me introduce my associate." I look over at Renee and give her a sideways head motion to come over.

Renee comes over and sits down as I get up and sit on the edge of the coffee table in front of them both. "Rodney, this is Renee. She handles the legal aspects of this operation. Renee, this is Rodney. He's interested in our operation."

"You a lawyer, Renee?" he asks as he looks her up and down.

I knew the hippy outfit was going to mess us up.

"Hi, Rodney. I am very convicted that the action in Vietnam is an illegal war by the United States. It is my mission to make sure that young men like you never have to violate their conscience by serving in the fascist military." She makes air quotes when saying, "serving."

"I want to get out of this be –"

I kick Rodney's foot and shake my head, "no" quickly to stop him. Renee doesn't give a hoot about why he wants out, but we have to play the game. I wish she'd told me this was going to be her line. We need to coordinate better in the future.

Renee continues as if he never made a sound, "I make sure that we have proper documentation of your mental condition." She has been very close to Rodney and now gently puts her hand on his knee. "You must understand that there are some people in this corrupt government that would not see eye to eye with us, don't you?"

"Uh, yes."

"Good. I will do everything in my power to make sure that they will not have the slightest concern when you make your appointment. When is that?"

Good going, Renee, he has totally forgotten that you didn't respond to his question about being a lawyer and has just agreed to con the draft board.

"Monday morning."

"Oh my, that's not very much time." Renee turns to me. "Darryl, do you think we could make room for Rodney? I would hate to see him drafted just because we have too many other clients."

"I don't know, Renee, we're pretty busy and haven't had a break except for tonight." I'm looking pretty sad now as I look down at the floor.

"Hey, if you can do this then I can pay extra to get it done by Monday!"

Ah, music to my ears; he hit two of my favorite notes, pay and extra. "What do you think, Renee? We could work tomorrow on Rodney and push Higgins out since he's not up until Wednesday. But that means we have to do a data intake first thing in the morning."

Rodney looks expectantly at Renee, nodding his head, "Yes".

Renee pauses, furrowing her eyebrows to look as if she's pondering the proposal. I'm sure she's internally jumping for joy; I know I am. Finally she nods, "Yes, that would work, but – Rodney, we'll need to have $500 cash up front and $500 after you've – passed – your physical." More air quotes, this time around "passed."

Whoa, Renee really knows what extra means. I hope she's read him right; that's a lot of cash, the most we've ever asked.

Rodney shakes his head, "No." Oh man, she asked too much. Then he says, "No problem. What time can you be here?"

"We'll be here at 8:00 sharp. You can get a good night's sleep with no worries, Rod." I stand up and Renee follows suit, as does Rodney. We are awkwardly close together between the couch and the coffee table. "I would like to stay but it's getting late and we have things to get ready for tomorrow."

Renee gives Rodney a big hippy love hug, "We'll take good care of you."

"Thanks so much. I can't say how much this means to me," says Rodney as he unwraps himself from Renee and wrings my hand.

We make a couple of more lame comments as Rodney walks us to the door. I grab my trench coat and umbrella. Renee still has her shawl on. It's still raining so we hustle on the way back to the car. Darn VW will still be cold before we get it parked and walk back to our apartment.

As soon as we're out of sight, Renee squeals, "Alright! We did it."

We hug and have a really long smooch before moving on to the car.

Chapter Two

I put a foot in the middle of Renee's back and push. "Turn off the alarm." She grabs the blankets and tries to hang on as she goes over the edge of the bed. Vile curses and promises of death arise from the mound of blankets and flesh on the floor.

"If you wouldn't insist on having the alarm on your side of the bed, this wouldn't happen," I counter. "Or, you could just wake up when the darn thing goes off." I get up and head for the bathroom, ignoring her pleas for help. As I do my thing and then splash some water on my face to try to wake up, I'm wondering why I'm in such a foul mood. Oh, yeah, we had to set the alarm at an ungodly hour of 5:00 AM on a Saturday no less. Geez, it's still dark out. Who in their right mind gets up at this time of day?

Renee barges into the bathroom, drops her nighty on the floor, steps into the rusty tub, pulls the shower curtain around, and turns on the water. More curses, this time directed at the building super because it takes forever to get hot water. "Tell me again why we had to get up this early," she yells.

"We have to get some paperwork ready for Rodney to sign and we need to be there early enough to make sure he doesn't have any cops ready to nab us. We can't be too careful." I finally get enough hot water in the sink to shave and now the mirror is steaming up from Renee's shower. Great!

I finish shaving and go back into the living room to wait for my chance to shower. While I'm waiting I throw the blankets on the bed and lift the Murphy bed up and close the doors on it. I then step into the kitchenette and start a pot of coffee. The steam heat hasn't come on yet and the radiator is cold so I plug in the electric heater across the room from the kitchen so we don't blow a fuse. Renee comes out of the bathroom wrapped up in towels so I go in and shower.

When I'm done, Renee is sitting at the pastel green, two by four-foot table. There has to be at least six layers of various colors of paint showing through the legs where they've been hit by chairs. I think the table would weigh ten pounds less if we scraped it down to wood. Since it came with the apartment, I'm not about to do that.

I step into the closet and get dressed. I'm going to keep the same image as last night so pick a plain button-down shirt. What color did I wear last night? Oh, yeah, light blue, I better make it green this time. When I'm dressed, I sit in our other wooden chair to see how far Renee has gotten with the paperwork.

"How's it going, Honey?" I ask.

"It looks like we have all the forms we need," she says as she slides a fold over to me.

I look at the folder with the two brass brads poking through the holes punched in the top of the forms. It looks real legal-like. I nod, "Yeah, good thing we keep several in stock or we'd be stuck for this morning." I pull my briefcase out from under the table and put them in.

"Let's get something to eat then move out." I get up and take two steps into the kitchen, open the frig to grab a carton of milk and put it on the counter, I turn around, get two Tupperware bowls out of the cupboard, and am standing two inches from Renee who already has them. We rub butts as she gets spoons and frosted cornflakes while I pour two cups of coffee. Closeness is one of the advantages of a small kitchen, if that's what you can call it.

After breakfast, we take the six-block hike to the VW's parking space. It's only a fifteen-minute drive to Capitol Hill via the Montlake Drawbridge. We drive past Rodney's house and look for any cars with exempt license plates. We circle a few more blocks before we're sure there aren't any cops in the area. It's now 6:45 so we park across the street and at the end of the block so we can keep an eye on the place until our appointment at 8:00. There isn't much activity in the neighborhood at this time of day on the weekend so we relax.

"So how far are we going to go with this one?" asks Renee.

"Let's see what he's got. If he can come up with $500 cash overnight, our research will have proven right. The county records show that he owns the house free and clear which is quite remarkable. He's not like our previous marks. Just poor college kids trying to avoid the draft. I think he's really rich." I'm still keeping a look out while talking so I don't see Renee's reaction. "What do you think?"

"Maybe we can stretch this out for a while. But blackmail is such an ugly word and dangerous too, if he gets fed up and rats us out."

"Yeah, that could get us into big trouble. I'm a bit concerned that if he is as well off as we think, he may be too smart to sign the papers, but if he does, we wipe his bank account before he knows what hit him." I glance at Renee to see that this suggestion doesn't seem to faze her. Are we taking another step deeper into a life of crime?

I wait as she ponders my suggestion. Finally she responds, "Hmm, you know, that is really tempting," another pause. "If we did that, we would have to move. It would have to be an awful lot of cash, enough for us to start over somewhere else."

Now I have to think about it. I turn over some things in my mind, like this is out and out robbery. I guess I still have some conscience. The Voice tells me to stick to the regular plan. I reply, "It would have to be an awful lot of money. But if we do take too much, he might not hesitate to point the finger at us. If it isn't too much, then he wouldn't be willing to expose his duplicity in cheating the draft. His wealth is probably the reason he doesn't want to go to 'Nam. Let's see what he has and how eager he is to let us have some of it."

"Pig alert on your right," says Renee as she slouches down in the seat.

I stiffen up as I spot the black-and-white but it doesn't turn down our street so I relax and Renee sits up. "I wish you wouldn't call them pigs. That's so – I don't know, it just isn't right."

Renee laughs, "You're in the wrong business, Darryl! Besides, it's just slang."

I just grunt. It still bothers me for some reason.

8:00 rolls around and we wait another forty-five minutes to see what happens. There isn't any movement in or out of the house so we figure there aren't any cops waiting inside. Just to be safe, we leave the briefcase in the car as we walk the half-block to the house, up the stairs and ring the bell.

A concerned looking Rodney opens the door. "OK, so I wasn't dreaming last night. I thought you were going to be here at 8:00."

"We need to be really careful about screening our clients, Rodney. Is there anyone else in the house with you?" I ask.

"Say what? What does that matter?" asks Rodney as he jerks his head back a bit and squints his left eye.

"I'll let you know if we can look around first. What you have asked us to do would not be appreciated by all people and we wouldn't want them to overhear our conversation and arrangements," responds Renee as she smiles sweetly.

"Oh," Rodney nods slightly and steps away from the door. "Come on in. I think everyone left last night but sometimes I have someone crash in a bedroom upstairs."

We do a walk-through of the house but don't find anyone. Wow, this house is bigger than I thought last night. Five bedrooms and a big game room in the basement with a full-size pool table. I'm really impressed with his office and the cool roll-top desk. Lots of papers and bookkeeping type ledgers. There's a large locked file cabinet.

He also has some really nice paintings in every room. I wonder if they are originals.

I even check out his bathroom off his master bedroom, just long enough to pick up a couple strands of his hair. I'll need these later.

"It looks like we're alone," I say. "I'll go back to the car and get the briefcase." He has a quizzical look which I answer, "It contains information that could be used against us if there were cops waiting for us."

"Oh, OK," he nods.

I go back to the car, get the briefcase, and come back.

We return to the living room which still has beer bottles and party trash lying around. He motions to the couch as he sits in a wingback chair.

He jumps up and kicks the chair, then moves to one on the other side of the couch. I just raise my eyebrows.

"Somebody spilled something on it. Good thing I have someone coming in to clean up this mess today. But let's get down to business. As I remember, you claim to be able to make it look like I'm unfit for the military and there won't be any questions, especially by any authorities."

I meet Renee's eyes and nod. This is a good sign, he obviously has plenty of money if he can throw a party like last night and then hire someone to clean up after him.

He looks at me then Renee and pauses briefly, "I need to know more about how you're going to do this. Last night, I wasn't processing things too well."

"You were drunk," says Renee very matter-of-factly.

"Well, I, uh, yeah," Rodney stammers.

"Fine, we have to go over this in detail and since we were up late last night getting things ready, we'd like to know if you have the $500 advance before we continue." If he was too drunk, he may not have remembered the financial arrangement.

"That's a lot of money," counters Rodney. He's looking just a little too stern right now.

I stand up. I'm not going to fool around negotiating but I also want to make sure he is eager enough. "Fine, if you don't feel it is worthwhile, we'll be on our way. We have other clients that we need to take care of."

"No, no, no, I didn't mean it that way. I'll get it right now." His demeanor changes as he stands and motions me to sit back down. He goes to his office and we can hear him open a drawer in his desk. He comes back with an envelope and hands it to me.

I look in the envelope and there are five crisp C notes in it. I put it down on the coffee table and put my briefcase beside it; I pop the snaps, open it, and lift out the legal folder.

"What we have here are medical documents that indicate that you had a serious head injury last winter. We've listed it from an accident during the cold snap in December. There was lots of ice so you slipped on the sidewalk. Unless you were out of town at that time this should hold up under a detailed review. This will explain to the draft board why you are incapacitated." I flip through the bottom four inches of documents that look just like the University of Washington Hospital's forms because that's where we got them. "The information on the documents has been copied from a person who did have a head injury. Any doctor who sees this will have no doubt about the authenticity of the diagnosis. We will need your full name to type on these, as well as your other vital statistics," I explain.

"OK, that's good, I remember the storm. Rodney P. McNairy."

"Could you spell your last name, Rodney?" asks Renee as she writes on a yellow legal pad. The yellow pad always impresses them.

"M, small c, Capital N, a, i, r, y," answers Rodney.

Renee then walks Rodney through the other questions getting his weight, height, and other things. He doesn't know his blood type.

Renee opens the briefcase and pulls out a manila envelope with pieces of cardboard with circles on them. Then she gets out a small bottle of rubbing alcohol and a cotton swab. She smiles at Rodney, "Give me a pinky."

Rodney warily reaches his hand toward her and before he knows it, she has stabbed his finger with a pin. "Yow! What is the hell?" He jerks his hand back.

Renee quickly grabs the finger, squeezes it to get blood on a toothpick, and spreads it on the circles. "You have type O positive blood, Rodney. Hold this cotton on your finger for a while."

"Geeze, how long have you been doing this?" he asks.

"Long enough to know what is needed to cover all the bases."

"So now let's go over the legal documents. These next documents are court appointed Power of Attorney giving me authority to intercede for you with the draft board, why I'm with you, and answer questions for you. Are you familiar with a Power of Attorney?" This is the one that could make or break the deal. If he completely understands its significance, giving me the right to liquidate everything he has and take it before anyone finds out, it could kill the deal.

Rodney's jaw drops, "Say what? How can I give you that? You could even sell my house if you wanted."

OK, he knows what a Power of Attorney is so now I've got to smooth it over. "Easy, Rodney, take a look at this. First of all, your name isn't on it yet. But even more important is that the judge's name is a fake and so is the signature. You aren't at risk because we would never be foolish enough to try to use it other than when we go to the draft board. I may not even have to show it to the draft board. Most times they just look at it and hand it back."

"Humph," he grunts, "I'm not too sure about that. What else do you have? I may want to come back to this."

"Certainly, we want to make sure that you're confident that this will work with minimal risks. The documents are there as back up but when they examine you, they will have no doubt that the documents are real." I sit back, trying to show how relaxed I am and not concerned about his concern.

"I'm not that good of an actor. How will they be convinced?"

I lean forward now to draw him in. "I have a secret Indian recipe that produces a temporary catatonic state. You will be semi-conscious for about 20 hours after it takes affect. Sunday evening, we will come over, give you the dose, and stay overnight to make sure you don't wonder off somewhere. In the morning, I'll take you to your appointment. I'll be with you until you come out of it Monday evening. At that time, your final $500 will be due."

"What happens if they try to question me, or give me a blood or urine test? Is this recipe going to expose me?"

I want to roll my eyes but don't dare. "If they question you, you will be able to answer a few questions but not very clearly. You won't be able to complete a sentence and make sense. As far as chemical tests, they won't find anything they've seen before. They're looking for weed, LSD, heroin, and stuff that's known to them. Since this isn't a street drug and doesn't give you a trip, they won't be testing for it."

"So what's in it?"

"Curiosity killed the cat, Rodney. If I told you then it wouldn't be a secret." I can't let this stuff get out, besides, I don't even know.

"Side effects?" he asks.

I shake my head, what's with this guy? I hope he isn't getting cold feet. I look him straight in the eye. "You will remember very little of anything that happens while you are under the influence. Some have had headaches the next day. The drug isn't approved by the FDA and it hasn't had field trials with control groups. All I can say is that it serves its purpose and I haven't had anyone want their money back."

"What happens if someone checks back with me or the hospital to verify my condition?"

"Now that's a good question. The draft board should send you notification of your status within two months. Remember these guys are a government bureaucracy. They only act fast when it is to their advantage. If they want to see you again, they'll send a letter. All you need to do is contact us and we'll help you out again.

"If they check with the hospital, well, we've arranged to have your records updated there. You are covered in any eventuality." I try to be as matter-of-fact as I can since Rodney is understandably nervous. The key is to make him think we have all bases covered, whether or not we do.

"Look, Darryl, this looks comprehensive and that you have everything thought out, but I'm still concerned about that Power of Attorney." Rodney is quite fidgety as he speaks. "Even if it is a fake, it looks real and a bank wouldn't have any problem granting you access to my accounts."

I glance at Renee for help and all I see on her face is, "Think fast Darryl, rent is due tomorrow."

Here I am running a scam on the government and trying to convince my mark I'm honest. Then it hits me. "Rodney, you're working with a couple of people here that the government wouldn't hesitate throwing in prison if they caught us. To them, we are criminals. I can tell you I'm not going to rip you off, but I'd rather earn your money and get you out of the draft. As Renee has said before, getting you out of the draft is our higher purpose, even if it is illegal."

Before he can say anything, Renee finishes it off. "Rodney, I've risked my freedom to help people like you because I believe this is what is right. This war is illegal and immoral. Our young men, the future of our nation, are getting killed and maimed for an unjust cause. We have no desire for riches; we simply need enough to keep the cause going." She gives him a sad smile that reeks with sincerity.

His frown softens a bit but I can tell he needs just a little more of a push.

"So, what we'll do is finish this paperwork today and bring it back to you. Since they won't accept anything but an original or a certified copy, which we can't get on either Saturday or Sunday, you will have the only copy in your possession and on Monday, it has to come with us. Monday evening, you rip it up or keep it in case we need it again. How does that sound?

"Your other option is for us to walk and you get drafted." That's it; I remind him of why we are here in the first place. I don't want him to think about the possibility of us going to his bank while he's still under the influence on Monday.

"OK, if you bring back the Power of Attorney when you finish it, I'll give you the first $500," responds a tightlipped Rodney as he picks up the envelope with the cash and flips it back and forth. The man's not a fool, just desperate.

I still try to maintain a relaxed exterior even though I would really like to see those bills in my hand instead of his. It crosses my mind that he could still be a snitch. $200 will cover rent and expenses for a while. I'll go for it.

"Rodney," I pause for effect, "we've already invested quite a bit of time, and you could get cold feet and back out before we get back. Give us $200 now and the rest when we come back. Otherwise, we're out of here." I need to be firm. I also consider not coming back even if he does give us the cash.

"Fair enough," he says as he hands over the envelope after taking three C notes out. "When will you be back?"

I look at Renee and she answers, "It's 10:00 now, and we have other business this afternoon, so I can finish the Power of Attorney and be back by 11:00. So we better get moving." She scoops up the folder and puts it back in the briefcase in one smooth motion, closing the lid and snapping the latches.

I like this woman! We think alike.

I reach out my hand to shake Rodney's as I get up. He returns the shake and Renee and I are out the door in a flash as I turn and say, "See you at 11:00."

As we return to the car I keep looking back to see if I can see if he's watching through the window. I can't see him and that could be a good sign. I don't want him making our car.

When we get to the car, Renee gets in the driver's side and rolls down the window. "Keep a good eye on him. I'm not sure I trust him yet and check to see if the bills are marked. I'll be back in a jiffy."

Renee leaves and I take up a position near a large maple tree to keep out of sight but where I have a view of the house and the streets. Time passes slowly at a time like this and I hope no neighbors get suspicious, one of the reasons to keep the time short. While I'm waiting, I also examine the bills with my magnifying glass. No hint of marking so far but I still use a cigarette lighter to carefully – very carefully warm the bills to expose any hidden ink. Still good, whew!

I see Renee return and park down the street from where we parked before. I wave an OK and she gets out of the car and comes up to my position.

"Any trouble?" she asks.

"Nope, no signs of any activity other than a normal neighborhood and no markings on the bills. I don't think he's a snitch, just more cautious than most."

"That's good, I was wondering if we should just make off with the $200 and forget him, but another $800 sounds better now," she says and gives me a peck on the cheek. "You did good."

The Voice says the same thing.

"I couldn't do it without you, Sweetie," I affirm as we walk back to Rodney's house and ring the bell.

We exchange the Power of Attorney for the three C notes and are on our way after letting Rodney know we will be back tomorrow at 8:00 PM.

The rest of the afternoon is a whole lot less tense. I find the landlord and pay our rent while Renee finishes typing Rodney's information in the medical records. The IBM Selectric typewriter was a super investment, or should I say acquisition. It would be hard to match the legal and medical documents without it.

Chapter Three

Sunday morning rolls around and we sleep in. Long gone are the days when I'd get up early and go to church. That didn't last long after I left home and found out how hypocritical the Catholic Church really was.

I don't know why I keep thinking about what happened when I was just out of Navy boot camp. I was stationed just outside of Memphis, Tennessee and going through aviation electronics training. Being a good Catholic, I went to Mass on Sunday and confession regularly. I chuckle to myself as I remember the day I told the priest that I had been swearing a lot lately. He replied that it was my military duty to keep a clean mouth. I was shocked.

I left the chapel wondering why a priest would tell me that it was military duty instead of a sin. Then I thought about the changes to Catholic rules and regulations that applied to me after I joined the Navy. I had been informed that eating meat on a Friday was now OK. I wasn't required to abstain from meat anymore, something about needing my strength? So I'm sitting on my behind in a training school five days a week and now I can eat meat on Fridays!

Man! I remember taking the hamburger out of a cheeseburger when I was a kid so I wouldn't have a sin on my soul. Now I shouldn't swear, not because it offends God, but because it's my duty. By the time I got back to the barracks, I decided that if sin wasn't always sin, then there was something wrong with this religion. That was the last time I went to church.

Now I don't think too much about what is right or wrong as long as I'm not hurting someone else. I figure that I can do just about anything I want and not get caught, which brings me back to the business of the day.

I think it's about time to get up so I reach over to see if Renee is awake. She isn't but after a few minutes of batting my hand away she gets the idea that I didn't really want to get up.

After brunch, we take a stroll up the Ave to buy supplies for my tonic. We go to our local apothecary, and even though it looks closed, I try the door and a little bell tinkles as it opens. The smell of sweet incense is heavy and the lights are much dimmer than the cloudy sky was outside.

Mary looks up from the counter with her long straight black hair falling over her shoulders. The beaded headband completes the picture of the brown-eyed Asian hippy. She just nods and smiles as we make sure there are no other customers in sight, then walk through the beaded curtain covering the door to the back room labeled, "Employees Only."

I blink my eyes a few times as it's even darker in the back room than it was in the main entrance to the store. As my eyes adjust, I can see an old Chinese guy sitting in an old wooden office chair with casters in front of a roll-top desk that must be 100 years older than he is. His denim vest with embroidered flowers and raggedy jeans don't fit his long gray ponytail. I wonder what they called him before there were hippies. He stands up as we walk in.

"Ah, good friend Darryl, and lovely Renee, how good to see you. What can I get you today?" he asks as he waves his hand toward the shelves surrounding us, all filled with jars and cans that appear to be as old as the desk.

"Hi, Joe, we just came in to visit today. It's been a while since we've seen you," I lie.

Joe bursts out laughing. He knows me too well.

Renee just rolls her eyes. We do this every time I come.

"Well, come, let's have some tea and we can talk about what you need while we catch up." He motions to a small table at the end of the room near a window with the shades pulled down. Joe brings a kettle of hot water as we sit down and prepares tea for us.

I wouldn't have guessed when I first met Joe that he has a pharmaceutical degree from the University of Washington. His involvement with naturopathic medication is strictly cultural, besides his branching out into more modern but unconventional drugs. He knows exactly what his products do to the human physiology. Everything he sells in his store is legal but rumor has it that he may have other outlets that may not be.

"How are you two kids doing? It's been a while since you've looked me up together."

I always want to be upbeat but there's no hiding things from Joe so I answer, "Not too good. We've been scraping by but haven't made any major scores."

"Yeah, but we may have a live one on our hands now," beams Renee.

"Oh, tell me about it," asks Joe as he cocks his head slightly toward her.

"He's a rich kid who wants to avoid the draft but got called up because he's been partying too much. Grades slipped and now he's up for a medical exam. Pretty standard for us except when I say rich. I think he's loaded and I mean loaded." I bob my head to make sure Joe understands how loaded. "He had five crisp C notes in his desk that we know about and probably more stashed somewhere."

"Hmm, not bad. I assume you're going to need the usual formula before his exam?" asks Joe.

I sip my tea and nod. "Yeah, but how are things with you? Store looks good, Mary looks good." Renee kicks me but I ignore it. "Business OK?"

"Excellent! The current peace movement is bringing a lot of people here who appreciate my brand of medicine. Word of mouth advertizing keeps more people coming in for what ails them." Joes winks knowingly.

We spend at least a half hour chatting before we get down to business. I take a small envelope from my pocket with the hairs from Rodney's bathroom and pass it to Joe.

Joe opens the envelope. "Ah, very good. These will do nicely. Let me prepare the formula for you." He gets up and goes to his workbench. He holds his chin as he looks across the top row of bottles on the shelf above the bench. He reaches up and pulls down several.

I watch with curiosity because there are no labels on the jars. He carefully measures out some of the ingredients on a balance scale, tipping the tray, and pouring the powder or crystals into a mortar. Soon, he is mixing and grinding it together with a pestle.

"His weight?" Joe asks without turning around.

"180," answers Renee. "I got that from his medical input."

"Excellent, my dear," he replies as he adjusts the weights on the scale and measures the powder and puts it in a vial. Next, he snips the hair into inch long pieces and adds three to a vial. With a pipette, he adds a few drops of a liquid from another bottle. There is a brief sizzle as they drop in. He adds a few drops from another liquid, swirls the mixture around, holds it up to the light, then puts a stopper in the vial.

He returns with the two vials, one with the liquid, and one with the powder. He sits down with us again. "I'm sure you know how to use this but tell me anyway."

"Between eight and sixteen hours before the exam, I will mix these two ingredients together. Once they stop bubbling, I'll mix it with two ounces of distilled water and give it to the subject to drink. After he passes out, I'll perform the incantation over him. After the exam, I'll perform the release incantation to bring him out of the spell." I wonder why he always asks me to do this, but I suppose I could mess it up.

"You have learned well. However, this time, wait until The Voice gives you the incantation," says Joe without any expression.

My eyes widen. I'm shocked. Joe has never mentioned The Voice in front of others before.

Renee looks at me with the what-is-he-talking-about look.

I stutter, "Ah, The Voice will tell me the incantation?"

The Voice tells me he will.

Joe's left eyebrow rises.

I say, "OK."

Renee grabs my arm, "What's The Voice?"

Joe nods but says nothing.

I sigh. I knew there would be a time to tell Renee but I certainly didn't expect it to be today. If she freaks out, that could be the end of this scam and possibly our relationship. But I haven't known The Voice to be wrong and he wouldn't have brought it up to Joe at this time if it wasn't important.

"Joe's knowledge of medicine has been passed down from the Shang dynasty by Chinese medicine men. Medicines and the soul or spirit have been connected for ages in these traditions. It incorporates yin and yang philosophy along with several Eastern religions. Joe has developed a connection with a spiritual being who advises him, just as he guided Joe's mentors.

"You know that Joe and I've know each other for several years, before I met you. During that time Joe has been teaching me about his spirituality. Well, about a month ago, I heard a voice inside my head. He whispers advice or encouragement to me every once in a while, not often. He led me to Rodney Friday night and he just confirmed to me that he would provide the incantation."

I sit back and cross my arms waiting to see what Renee will say.

She looks at Joe then at me. I think it is disbelief on her face. I can't really tell. Finally she looks at Joe and asks, "Is this Voice the same one that you have a connection with? Do you hear a voice also?"

Joe slowly nods his head, "Yes, I hear his voice too. He is the one who guides me when I make up the formula. He has given me the incantation that Darryl has used in the past. This is the first time he has told me that he will give the incantation directly to Darryl."

"So this must be part of that meditating thing you started." She shakes her head. "You guys are either crazy or have stumbled on a gold mine," says Renee. She doesn't look happy but then, she isn't running out the door screaming either. "I sure hope your – Voice – doesn't get us in trouble," she continues, making air quotes around "voice."

I can tell she's still thinking about it. I know her well enough to know she's trying to figure out how this will affect our ability to make scores, as well as our relationship. OK, that's what I'm wondering too.

We leave the apothecary and as soon as we're on the street Renee hits me on the shoulder, hard, too.

"Ouch, what the hell is that for?"

"When were you going to tell me about this Voice thing?" she demands.

"I don't know. You don't tell me everything that's going on in your head, do you?" I counter.

"No, but this is a whole lot bigger than thinking about stuff, it's beyond philosophy, it's, it's," Renee stops apparently searching for a word. "It's spiritual and that could mean – I don't know – and that's what bothers me, that and you didn't trust me with it."

Ah, that's the real problem. She thinks you don't trust her. That was The Voice in my head.

I have a momentary train of thought, more like a train crash of thoughts run through my mind. The Voice is talking to me more and more. It makes me a bit nervous but he's right. Do I trust Renee? Why should I? She's a con artist just like me, maybe better. I've seen her work marks.

I stop in the street and face Renee, put my hands on her arms and look her in the eye. Somehow I know this is the way The Voice would want me to do it. "I'm sorry, I should have told you about this, but it's happening so fast now. What was just some meditation and relaxing stuff Joe was teaching me has suddenly escalated in just the past few days and there has to be a reason for it.

"The Voice knows we're a team. I think he brought this out into the open so we can work together even better. We live together, we have fun together, and I love you. The Voice isn't going to change any of that," I reassure her.

Renee takes a deep breath and puts her arms around me. I rest my chin on her head. "I love you too, Darryl, even if you are a con artist." We just stand there as people walk by, then she adds, "And you better not be conning me!"

I laugh, "No way, Babe." As we turn and start walking back down the Ave with my arm around Renee, I reveal some of my impressions about what's going to happen. "I would like to say that this is what The Voice is saying, but this is more of a gut feeling. I know for sure, he led me to Rodney. I think he is leading us into the most important score we have ever made. This is going to take us places we never dreamed we could go. This is only the beginning."

She looks up at me and smiles, "That certainly sounds good!"

Chapter Four

It's 8:00 PM, the sun has just gone down and it's time to get Rodney prepared for his physical in the morning. Still being cautious, we park away from the house and walk up the sidewalk. As we step up on the porch, we can hear a woman yelling inside.

"I hope this doesn't mean trouble for our little project," I comment as I reach for the brass lion-head doorknocker.

"It sounds like a ticked off girlfriend," replies Renee. "We can't let her stay around for the procedure."

Before I can knock, the door is flung open and there is a knock-out gorgeous chick with one of the meanest scowls on her face that I've ever seen. "Out of my way!" she screams and starts moving as I barely have a chance to move aside.

We both turn and watch her charge down the steps and through the gate.

"I guess it's not going to be a problem getting rid of her," I say calmly as we turn back to find Rodney standing at the door. Oh, I'm embarrassed about my choice of words.

"Why would you want to get rid of her? She's my fiancée," he asks.

"I didn't really mean to get rid of her, like never see her again. It's just we don't want anyone around while we prepare you for tomorrow. With all the yelling, it wouldn't work," I try to explain.

"Yeah, whatever, come on in," says Rodney, obviously not in a good mood. He picks up a manila envelope off the sitting bench. "I need to put this away; I'll be back in a minute." He goes into his office and I can hear him open a safe and close it. I don't remember seeing a safe there last night.

"Can I get you guys anything? Beer maybe?" he asks as he heads for the kitchen. "I sure could use one."

"Hey, Rodney, remember we asked you not to eat or drink anything after noon except for water?" I call to him.

Rodney does a little skip on one foot and turns away from the kitchen. "Yeah, that's right. I almost forgot. Sydney's gotten me a bit upset. So I guess we might as well get started. Where do you want to do this?"

"The living room is just fine. We have everything we need in my purse and the couch looks comfortable enough as long as we can turn the lights down," answers Renee as she walks to the couch and starts taking things out of her black handbag. There's the two vials that we'll need to mix, next comes a small glass for the water, and then a small bottle of distilled water.

"Have a seat on the couch, Rodney. You'll probably feel dizzy after you take the potion and lying down will help." I explain as I pull a wingback chair closer and sit down.

Rodney sits down beside Renee while I take the vial with the liquid and pull the stopper. I hold it up to the light as if I'm making sure it's the right stuff. All for show. I take the lid off the vial with the powder. Slowly, I pour the clear liquid into the white powder and hold it at eye level and watch it fizz. A slight greenish haze rises from the bubbling broth.

Rodney appears captivated by the sight as his jaw drops open slightly. "You're sure this stuff is safe?" he asks weakly.

"Absolutely positive," I answer as I recap the vial when the fizzing stops. I shake it up to make sure all the powder is dissolved. The solution is now a dark green. I'm guessing there may not be much in there except white vinegar, baking soda, and whatever it takes to make it turn green. Maybe something to help him sleep also.

Renee has already measured out two ounces of water into the glass and I hand the vial to her. She uncaps it and pours the green liquid into the water and swirls it around until it is a consistent light green. She hands the glass to Rodney and says, "Here's to the end of the draft. Bottoms up, Rodney."

Rodney takes it in his right hand and gingerly looks at it at arm's length. He hesitates then gulps it down.

Renee gets up and turns down the lamps in the room.

"Good job, Rodney," I say as I look at my watch. "In about two minutes you will start to feel very sleepy. At that time you will want to lie down. You will fall into a deep sleep but you will still be able to hear everything I say. Do you understand?"

"I'm feeling dizzy now, yes, I understand. I want to lie down," he responds slowly as he stretches out on the couch.

I continue to talk to him in a low smooth voice, "Focus on my voice, Rodney, you are feeling sleepy, your eyes are getting heavy, you can't keep them open, keep listening to my voice." I repeat this several times until I'm sure he is pliable.

"Rodney, answer me only when I ask you a question. Do you understand?"

Rodney replies groggily, "Yes, I understand."

"Now listen to me carefully. I'm going to repeat some Chinese words that will sooth your spirit." I need those words now, Voice.

Let me speak the words through you.

Say what? I thought you would tell me and I would repeat them.

Just empty your mind and let me control your vocal cords. Relax, you have nothing to fear.

Oh my gosh, I don't really have a choice, we've come this far. OK, go ahead.

I close my eyes and I can feel them rolling back under my eyelids. I start speaking something that sounds like Chinese. I repeat the rhythmic repetitive words several times.

Your turn.

I open my eyes and look at Rodney. He appears to be asleep. "Rodney, repeat what I just said."

Slowly, Rodney repeats the phase The Voice had said through me.

"Very good, Rodney. When I snap my fingers, you will wake up but you will obey me and you will not remember anything we say until I tell you. You will not feel dizzy and you will not feel sleepy. When I clap my hands three times, you will fall back into a trance. Do you understand?"

"Yes, I understand," he replies.

I look at Renee and she nods to go ahead.

I snap my fingers and Rodney opens his eyes and looks at me. "Huh, how long was I asleep?"

"It's only been a couple of minutes. How do you feel?" I ask. I need to run some test to see how well the spell is working.

"I feel fine. The dizziness has passed." He starts to sit up.

"Don't get up."

Rodney lies back down.

"What is your social security number, your bank's name, your checking account number, and your mother's maiden name?" I ask. If that doesn't scare him out of the spell, nothing will.

Rodney calmly tells me his social security number and the National Bank of Commerce. He hesitates and I wonder if he will go on, but he continues to give me everything I asked. He starts to ask, "Why do you – ?"

I clap my hands three times and he closes his eyes and doesn't complete his question. Renee gives me a thumb up.

"Rodney, the next time you wake up, you will have difficulty speaking, you will talk and act like a four-year-old child but you will obey Renee and me completely. You will drag your left foot slightly when you walk and turn it outward. You will have difficulty using your left arm. You will remain under my control at all times. Do you understand?"

Again Rodney replies that he understands so I snap my fingers and he wakes up. He looks around with a bewildered look on his face. "Wh-here am I?" he asks stuttering and obviously having trouble talking. "Wh-oo are you, wh-where's my mom and dad?"

"Easy Rodney, I'm Darryl and this is Renee. Your mother and father asked us to take care of you while they had to go on a trip by themselves.

"Would you go into the kitchen and get a glass of water for Renee, please?" I ask to see how well he does with his new handicaps as well as obedience.

"OK." He gets up and limps to the kitchen dragging his left foot slightly. He comes back in a minute with a glass of water in his right hand and gives it to Renee.

Renee takes the glass. "Why, thank you, Rodney. But I don't need this right now. Please take it back to the kitchen."

"OK," he answers as he reaches for it with his right hand.

"No, Rodney, use your left hand," says Renee.

Rodney tries to reach for the glass with his left hand, then uses his right to help his left reach and hold the glass. He takes it back to the kitchen.

"I think he has passed the tests. What do you think?" I ask Renee.

"I think we have a winner. There's no way those military doctors are going to be able to give him anything other than 4-F. Tomorrow at this time, we'll have our cash and be on our way," she says with a wiry smile.

"Well, it's past 9:00; let's put our kid to bed and get ready for tomorrow." I'm thinking that I really don't want to deal with a four-year-old right now.

Rodney comes back from the kitchen and I tell him it's time to go to bed.

"I'm h-hungry," he protests.

That's right, he didn't eat anything since noon. "OK, let's see what you have in the kitchen." I shrug my shoulders at Renee who starts laughing.

We manage to find some peanut butter and jelly along with some Wonder bread. Rodney seems to know what a four-year-old really wants before bedtime. He also wants to stay up later, typical of other clients I've had. I tell him firmly to go to bed and he does. I'm sure glad I told him to obey. I would hate to have to deal with a real four-year-old.

After Rodney is put to bed, Renee and I grab a beer and relax on the couch for a while.

"Wouldn't it be cool if we kept Rodney under the spell?" asks Renee. "Just think of what we could do with his riches." She kicks off her shoes and puts her feet up on the coffee table.

"I have no idea how long the spell lasts or how much he has. What happens when it wears off and he finds out we took him to the cleaners?" I ask, hypothetically interested.

"While you were putting our baby to bed, I was snooping in his office. You won't believe what I found," she teases.

"I'll play along, what did you find?" I roll my eyes. Two can play this game.

She hits me on the arm, "Come on, you want to know, don't you?"

I turn to look directly at her, "Well this must be really good. You usually go a couple more rounds before hitting me."

Her eyes get big and she nods quickly, "It really is. He has over $100,000 in his bank account, a few million in stocks, this house free and clear, as we knew already, along with some other properties."

"Wow! He left that much information out in the open for you to find? I thought he was more cautious than that."

"No, Silly, some of it was locked up in his wall safe and file cabinets," she laughs.

"I don't remember seeing a safe, where was it and how –," I don't get a chance to finish.

"I was looking for the keys to the file cabinets and found the combination to the safe taped under the middle drawer of his desk, too common of a place to keep your combo. The safe is hidden behind the Van Gogh beside his desk. Once I had that, the keys to the file cabinets were in the safe. And get this; it was all an inheritance. His parents were killed a couple of years ago in a car accident and he is an only child. So what do you think?" asks Renee, obviously quite proud of herself.

I sit back on the couch and put on my pursed-lip-seriously-thinking face. I start slowly, "It sure sounds like it might work if we could keep him out of it. That's the big if. We've always seen the spell wear off even when we don't tell them to wake up." Renee just looks at me as if I should say something more.

"I suppose we could call Joe and find out if we can give him another dose before this one wears off," I finally offer.

"That's a good idea. Why don't you call him now? If he goes along with it, I can get it while you take Rodney for his exam tomorrow," responds Renee.

She's obviously eager to do more on this one. I'm not comfortable with this and getting more uneasy as we talk about it. But I don't want to cross her at this point in the venture either. I get up and go to the phone in Rodney's office.

I have to laugh, he has one of those lighted dial princess phones with push buttons instead of rotary dial, a real sissy phone. I dial and wait but get a disconnected message instead of Joe. I think I must have misdialed and try again, carefully pushing each button to make sure I have the right number as well as trying to listen for a single tone with each push. What a stupid design for a phone, putting the dial mechanism in between the earpiece and the microphone so you can't hear the tone while you press it. It'll never catch on.

Once more I get the disconnected message. I go to the kitchen which has a wall phone. Thankfully it is a rotary, this time. I dial the number and again get a disconnected message.

I go back into the living room and shake my head, "I tried to call three times and got a disconnected message each time. I'm puzzled why he would have the phone disconnected. We were just there and no indication that he was changing his home phone number."

"It's probably the phone company's fault," replies Renee. "I'll go up to the store tomorrow while you take care of Rodney and meet you back here."

Renee gives me a coy glance and finishes the last of her beer. "You know, I'm kind of eager to crawl into one of those fancy beds in one of Rodney's guest rooms. You never know how different one of those beds might feel," she says with a wink.

"Best offer I've heard since this morning."

Chapter Five

I wake to the clanging of the windup alarm clock at 5:00 AM. What a horrid hour for anyone to get up! But getting Rodney to his 8:00 AM appointment is much more important than being able to sleep in later. I grope in the dark and knock the noisy menace on the floor. It's still ringing.

"Darryl, would you shut that thing off!"

"I think it rolled under the bed. Can you get the light?" I'm now on my hands and knees looking for the alarm. Thankfully I'm not blinded when Renee finally finds the light switch on the lamp on her side of the bed. A strange room and furniture is around me as I grab the alarm and stand up. Oh, yeah, I remember, this was the third bed we finally decided to crash in.

"It looks like this room has its own shower. I'll be out in a minute," I say as I head for the bathroom.

"One of the others did too. I'll try one of those," I hear Renee say as I close the door.

After a nice hot shower, I see that Rodney has the guest rooms well equipped for unexpected guests. He has some of those new disposable razors, shaving cream, deodorant, and some other stuff that I suppose a woman would use. I take my time, but don't want to dawdle; there's no telling how long it will take to get Rodney ready.

I come back in the bedroom and find Renee getting dressed. I put on my pants and go downstairs to get my more dress up clothes that I'll wear to accompany Rodney. I don't want to look like a hippy but a professional caretaker. I dress downstairs and then go back up to get Rodney.

I enter his room to find he's still fast asleep waiting for my command to wake him up.

"All right Rodney; it's time to wake up."

I'm pleased to see Rodney stir and wake up. He throws his covers off and jumps out of bed. "Wh-what's for br-breakfast? I'm h-hungry. Wh-what are we going to do t-today? Can I w-watch cartoons this m-morning?" he asks with difficulty but a lot of enthusiasm.

"Don't overdo it Rodney. It's Monday and there aren't any cartoons on this morning. You get into the bathroom and take a shower." He hobbles toward the bathroom. "Take some clean underwear with you," I remind him and he goes back to a dresser and gets some briefs and heads back to the bathroom. "Five minutes maximum," I shout as he closes the door. I wonder if they had cartoon on TV when he was four, or is that what he did as an adult. I'm always a little leery of telling someone to act like a four-year-old, but haven't had any major problem yet.

After just five minutes, I hear the shower stop. He probably wore his watch in the shower and stared at it the whole five minutes. I wait a minute or so and then open the door. He's standing in front of the mirror staring at himself.

"Anything wrong, Rodney," I ask.

"I-I don't know. I think I sh-should be doing s-something else but I don't know wh-what," he stammers.

"You need to shave. You do know how to do that, don't you? And put on some deodorant too." He turns around and looks at me as if I had just spoken in Chinese.

"Fine, Rodney, you will remember how to shave and put on deodorant," I use my authoritarian voice to make sure he complies.

I have to make sure Rodney gets dressed and behaves during breakfast. By the time we're almost ready to leave, I'm pretty sure that no amount of money could compel me to keep Rodney under this spell. It might be a bit easier if he were the same size as a four-year-old but I remind myself that he obeys better than one.

I ask Rodney where his car keys are and he leads me into the office, opens a drawer on the desk, and brings out the keys.

"Thanks, Rodney. Go get in the car and wait for me. I need to talk with Renee and I'll be downstairs in a minute."

"O-K, Mr. Da-rryl, see-ee yo-u there," replies Rodney as he opens the door to the stairs and awkwardly makes his way down.

I watch and am amazed how well a human brain can adapt to suggestions as Rodney hangs on to the handrail with both hands and moves down sideways, always making sure his weight is on his right foot and very little on his left.

Renee comes down the stairs from the bedroom.

"Do you have enough cash to get another dose?" I ask. "We may have to work a deal with Joe. $50 a day is a lot if we want to keep this up." Between rent, Joes' fee, and paying Martin to update Rodney's files at the U's medical center, I wasn't sure how much we had left of the first $500.

"Yeah, I still have about $150 left. Do you have parking money? It's amazing how quickly our expense mount up for a job like this," she answers. "I'll be back here by 10:30 so I'll see you when you roll in."

I give her a hug, "I have ten bucks for parking. I love you, see you later. It shouldn't be much after 12:00 at the latest. I can't imagine them wanting to keep Rodney much longer than an hour or so, but you know how the government works."

I go down the stairs into the basement garage. Unlike many of the houses in the area, this garage is still used for a car. When I step into the small garage, I know why he keeps it. He has a classic '53 Corvette, one of only 300 handmade cars. This guy may have even more cash than we imagined.

I stop gaping at the car when I see Rodney in the driver's seat. "Get in on the passenger side, Rodney. You are in no condition to drive."

"Aww, sh-shucks," he complains as he gets out and goes to the passenger side.

I press the garage door opener button on the wall and get in the car. What a difference from a junker VW bug. I start the car, slip it into drive, and carefully accelerate up the ramp to the street. He has a remote on the visor for the garage door and I watch it in the mirror as it closes.

I take 23rd south to East John and follow it until it turns into Olive Way and on into downtown Seattle. I decide to park in the Nordstrom's parking garage. It's only a block from the draft board's medical exam location.

We walk slowly to the building. Rodney's looking around as if it's the first time he's ever been here. Good work, Rodney. We enter the building and I get this déjà vu feeling like I've been here before. Oh, wait, I get the same feeling every time I bring in a client. It reminds me of my NROTC exam when I was in high school. Fortunately, I flunked that physical or I'd still be stuck in the Navy serving as an officer, that is if I'd made it through college or an enlisted man if I'd flunked out.

The ease with which I messed up that physical by answering a couple of questions the wrong way gave me the idea to start this business. This is much surer than the first few guys I coached. Not all of them pulled it off.

We get off the elevator into a foyer which opens up right into the waiting room. There are maybe twenty guys sitting around waiting to be called. We get into line to sign in with the receptionist. I'm a little nervous as I recognize her from the last time I was here. The Voice tells me to relax, there won't be any problems.

Rodney is starting to fidget but I let him. It works better that way. We inch forward as each person is asked the same bunch of questions then told to sit down and wait.

Finally it's our turn. We both step forward and the receptionist frowns, "Only one person at a time please." She looks back and forth at us, probably expecting one of us to step back.

"I'm with him." I point to Rodney. "I'm his caretaker."

She stares at me. "Weren't you in here just a few weeks ago with someone?" she asks.

"Yeah, I think so. We have several handicapped people we take care of. I'm the lucky one to bring them for their physical." I scoff, "To think the Army thinks they can draft these guys." I put on my you-guys- are- really-stupid look for her.

"Oh yes, I remember the attitude. So what's his name?" she asks.

"Tell her your name." I touch Rodney on the arm to get his attention.

"M-my n-name is Ro-dney," he says, then grins.

Receptionist has a hard time but I can see her trying not to roll her eyes, "Middle and last name, Rodney?"

Rodney looks at me, "Go ahead, Rodney, you know your name."

He hesitates then stammers, "Ro-dney Pee-ee Mc-Nairy." He laughs, "P-ee is my m-iddle na-me."

I shake my head. "No, Rodney, your middle name is Paiden."

He wrinkles his nose, "W-ell th-there's a na-me I'll n-ever use."

The receptionist just looks at me as I snicker, "You, what's-your-name, does he have his draft id with him?"

"Name's Smith. And, I brought his id." I hand it to her.

She takes it and looks at it, then compares it to a computer printout. Without looking up, she says, "Take a seat. Next."

The place looks more like a bus terminal than a waiting room. Mostly vinyl covered bench seats with chrome plated pipe arms. There are a few matching chairs as well. We find a seat near the door where guys have been disappearing after their names have been called. There is barely enough room for us.

I lean over and whisper to Rodney, "Pick your nose and wipe your fingers on your pants near the guy sitting next to you."

Rodney makes a big show of it. Even though he's acting like a four-year-old, there is an adult's brain behind it all.

It doesn't take long before the guy next to him gets up and moves to another location. Rodney's constant squirming helped too.

Time drags slowly. They don't even have magazines for us to read. I have to tell Rodney not to wander around the room as he gets up often like he would leave it given a chance.

Finally, they call Rodney's name. The guy at the door asks me where I think I'm going and I have to explain to him that I'm Rodney's caretaker.

"I don't care who you are, Mister, but this is Mr. McNairy's physical and we don't need you. You can wait here," says the guy.

"OK, I'll be right out here when you need me because Rodney won't cooperate with you unless I'm with him. He trusts me," I say loud enough for Rodney to hear, even though he's already through the door.

The door closes in my face and I laugh. It won't be long. I turn around to see a lot of faces staring at me. If it wasn't too late for these guys I could pass out my card and make a ton of money.

Two minutes later the door opens and the same guy points at me, "You, get in here."

"Excuse me; I'm not here for a draft physical. My name is Mr. Smith and you can address me properly." I don't budge but glance at the receptionist. Yeah, she remembers this part of attitude as she tries to keep from laughing.

The guy turns beet red but composes himself and says with strained calmness, "Mr. Smith, we require your assistance with your, ah, client. Would you please help us?"

I jump up all cheery and say, "I'd be glad to help." He holds the door open for me then leads me down a hall with curtains covering some of the cubicles and others were open. There were a couple of open ones with draftees sitting in their smocks.

We come to one and he pulls the curtain back. Rodney is standing there with his arms folded, a scowl on his face and fully dressed. The guy says to me, "We need him to take everything off, put on a smock and give us a urine sample."

"Mr. D-arryl, do y-ou kn-ow what they to-ld me? They to-ld me to ta-ke off mmm-y clothes and pee-ee in that jj-ar. I'm not going to that!" He shakes his head. "Tha-at wou-ldn't be nn-ice."

I turn to the guy, "Give me a minute." I pull the curtain. It's pretty close in here with just the two of us. I whisper to Rodney that it's OK to do what they want while I'm with him as long as he looks at me first and I nod. Then I say aloud, "It's OK, Rodney, they told you how to put on the smock and take the jar to the bathroom, didn't they?"

Rodney answers, "Yy-es. Bb-ut they ca-lled it a ggg-own. I not ww-ear a dr-ess."

I assure Rodney it is a smock then step outside and close the curtain.

The guy asks, "Is he always like this? What happened to him?"

"Slipped on the ice. Hit his head. Almost killed him," I say matter-of-factly.

"I'm sorry, I've seen some fakers here, but nothing like him. What's he doing here?" he asks, actually looking sympathetic.

"It seems the system doesn't always get the news so he got a draft notice." I shake my head in disbelief. "It's not the first time here for me. I've had to escort several of my clients here to prove they are incapacitated."

Rodney opens the curtain and stands there with the jar in his hand. I look at the guy and he points to the bathroom. "Have him come back here when he's done and we'll take him to a doc right away."

I walk down the hall with Rodney, open the door, and look in. There is a little window with a door in it. The sign above it says to open the door and put the jar on the shelf on the other side. I explain that to Rodney and leave him in the room.

I lean against the wall by the door and listen. Sure enough, he's messing around in there. I knock on the door, "Don't be messing around in there, Rodney, just pee in the jar and do as you were told then wash your hands and come out."

When Rodney comes out, I look in to see six feet of toilet paper on the floor and a half dozen paper towels scattered around, not to mention little puddles. "Boy, are they going to want to get rid of you. Follow me."

I lead Rodney back toward his cubical when the guy comes around a corner. "Mr. Smith, we're ready for you in exam room seven down this hall."

We go toward the exam room as I hear the next draftee to use the bathroom swear and yell that someone needs to clean up before he's going to use it.

He leads us into room seven then tells Rodney to sit on the exam table. Rodney looks at me and I nod so he gets up and sits down on the table. "The doc will be here in just a few minutes," says the guy as he leaves the room and closes the door.

Rodney twiddles his thumbs and kicks his legs. He lies down then sits back up. He's still doing well under the spell. He keeps on fidgeting until I hear a knock on the door and the doc enters.

This doc must have just gotten out of med school. I think he's younger than me. He must have barely passed as doctor if this is his first assignment.

"So Bert tells me that," he looks at his chart, "Rodney, here had an accident and is not himself. You're his escort for this physical?" he asks me.

"That's right, Doc," I reply.

"Well, we'll see. I've seen draft dodgers try all sorts of stuff before, but this is the first time they've brought an accomplice along," he says as he looks me in the eye.

I know he's trying to rattle Rodney or me. Fortunately, the spell will keep Rodney in line. The Voice tells me to give him the evil eye. What's that? I don't flinch but stare him down. He looks a bit discombobulated, turns away, and approaches Rodney. Oh, that was odd.

"OK, Mr. McNairy, I'm going to look at your eyes." The doc lifts a pen light toward Rodney's eyes and Rodney closes them. "We don't have time for this nonsense. Open your eyes right now," demands the doc.

"N-no."

I calmly tell Rodney to cooperate with the doc.

"O-OK, Mr. D-Darryl, if you say so." Rodney opens his eyes.

The doc gives me a dirty look then goes back to examining Rodney. He flashes the light in his right eye a couple of times and snorts, "Normal." He then does the left eye. He hesitates then does it again. The doc mumbles something under his breath then takes Rodney's right hand and tells him to squeeze. "Good grip." Then he takes his left hand and tells him to squeeze. The doc mumbles again.

Next he lifts Rodney's left arm straight in front of him and tells him to hold it steady. As soon as he lets go, Rodney's arm starts to drop so he reaches over with his right to hold it steady.

"You can let it down now," says the doc as he takes out his little rubber hammer. He deftly taps Rodney's right knee and gets a jerk. He tries the left and doesn't get much.

He then puts his stethoscope in his ears. As soon as he does, Rodney suddenly grabs the other end and yells, "Hhh-hi, Dd-oc," into it.

I'm trying not to laugh as the doc rips the stethoscope out of his ears. He is really angry, red face and the whole bit. Rodney doesn't hold back but burst out laughing. The doc doesn't say another word, just grabs his clipboard and leaves the room swearing.

Rodney is still sitting on the exam table and starts swinging his legs when his heel hits the metal base, it makes a hollow bonging sound. His eyes light up and he bangs it again. I think it's too bad he doesn't have rhythm; it would make a good drum. I let him bang away.

A minute later, Bert pokes his head in the door, "Mr. Smith, can you get Rodney to stop the noise?"

I lie, "I've tried, but he doesn't always respond."

Rodney grins and kicks harder.

Bert shakes his head and closes the door.

I wait about thirty seconds and tell Rodney to stop. I can only put up with it so long myself. "Good job, though, Rodney," I add.

Rodney grins again and gives it one last kick. That last kick bothers me a bit, as it is evidence of his ability to fight back against the spell.

Another five minutes pass and Bert sticks his head in the room again. "You can go back to the dressing room and get dressed. The exam is over. As soon as he's dressed, you can follow the exit signs. There is a check out desk and they'll give you more instructions if there is a need for any other tests. Good luck, Mr. Smith; I don't envy your job."

We go back to the cubical and Rodney puts on his clothes. Next we head down the hall away from the waiting room, around a couple of corners and come to the exit. There's a stern-faced old woman at the desk. I wonder why most people here seem to have an unwelcoming countenance.

She barely looks up, "You must be Rodney P. McNairy."

"Th-ats mm-ee, R-Rodney Pee," snickers Rodney.

The stern old lady shudders and hands me a sheet of paper. "Mr. Smith, the doctor has a preliminary conclusion that Mr. McNairy is 4-F. However, if the results of the urine tests reveal any traces of hallucinogens, there will be a follow up exam after a period of incarceration. If he appears to be normal at that time, you may both find yourselves in unpleasant places. You should receive a follow up notice or confirmation of 4-F in two or three weeks."

She has the witch routine down quite well. The previous people at the desk weren't quite as blunt and not as intense. I can tell she hopes Rodney will test positive.

The Voice says to use the evil eye again.

I don't really do much in the way of staring at her; I just meet her gaze and don't turn away. She immediately stiffens in her chair. She is visibly shaken and stammers, "I, ah, I'm ss-orry. Pl-ease g-go n-now."

Wow, this evil eye thing is quite powerful. I'm not sure what to make of it. It certainly disarms people.

We turn and go out the exit door. It leads us back into the foyer right beside the point where we got off the elevator. We retrace our steps to the parking garage and have to pay $2.50. What a robbery!

The trip back to Rodney's house is uneventful and I back the car down the ramp into the garage.

Chapter Six

When we get back upstairs, Renee greets me at the stairway door. "Darryl, we need to talk, alone," she whispers in my ear as she gives me a hug.

"Rodney, go to the kitchen and fix us all a lunch. And don't act like a four-year-old while you're doing it. You can use your left hand without any problem." Besides being hungry, I'm testing Rodney to see how well the spell is still working. If it wears off too much, he may not be willing to take the next potion.

"Oo-kay, Mr. D-darryl," replies Rodney as he shuffles off to the kitchen.

"Good, he kept the stutter and the lame foot," I say to Renee as he leaves the room. "Now, what's the problem?"

Renee takes a deep breath, "You'd better sit down."

We walk to the couch. I can tell something is wrong. Renee appears shaken, almost as much as the stern old lady after the evil eye thing. I wait for her to talk after we sit down.

"I'm scared, something is awfully wrong," she says. "I went to the apothecary and it wasn't there." She shakes her head.

"What do you mean it wasn't there?" I ask.

"I didn't really notice when I approached the store, but when I opened the door, it was all different inside. No incense, no Mary, bright lights, and no beaded curtain on a door to the back room. It's a used book store." Renee looks at me and I can sense she's pleading with me to believe her and not call her crazy.

I feel my mouth fall open but don't say anything for a few seconds. I'm trying to get my head around this. "I, uh, well, there has to be a logical reason for this," I try to sound convinced. "Did you ask anyone in the store about Joe?"

"Yeah," her head bounces up and down, "what do you think? I ask a clerk where Joe is and she says, 'Joe who?' I say the Chinese guy who owns the store and she gets all wrinkled nose and question marks all over her face and says, 'Henry Blake is the owner of the store. Would you like to talk to him?' So I ask her how long he's owned it and she says, 'Like as long as I've worked here, six months, but I don't know how long before that.' At that point I just leave and go outside. I look at the door and sure enough, it says 'HB Used Books' above the door. Not only that, the sign isn't new, it's dirty. The number on the door is still the same as when it was Joe's apothecary." Renee finally takes a breath.

I don't know what to think. Even if Renee was high when she went to the apothecary, she wouldn't imagine something this farfetched.

"Say something!" pleads Renee.

"I don't know what to say. How can a place we've frequented for over a year suddenly disappear and be replaced by a book store?"

"So you believe me?" she asks.

"Well, yeah, why wouldn't I? It wouldn't make sense to make up something this ridiculous." A strange thought entered my mind as I said that. Someone had said something like that to me once. Oh yeah, I remember.

I was arguing with someone about religion. The guy was telling me that Jesus was actually God in human form (something the Catholics said too) but he went on to say that God planned Jesus' death to pay for our sins because we couldn't pay for them ourselves. The only way to heaven was to accept Jesus' death in place of our eternal punishment for sin. I had said that was just crazy and he said that it was true and mankind wouldn't ever come up with a plan that ridiculous for salvation; only God would. What if he was right?

"Darryl, are you there?" asks Renee as she waves her hand in front of my face.

"Huh, yes, I'm here, I just had a horrible thought from my past about religion." I try to force the thoughts from my mind.

"Do you think this is something spiritual?" she asks.

"You know, you might be right," I answer, still trying to make sense of it. "I'll tell you what, why don't we drive up to Joe's house and see what we can find out?" I suggest.

"Finally, something that makes sense," breathes Renee.

Rodney comes into the room with a tray. It has three plates with sandwiches on them and three beers. "L-lunch is ser-ved."

"Thanks, Rodney. You only have to have problems speaking when someone beside Renee or me is around or might overhear us. I'm getting tired of the stuttering."

"Whew, thanks, I was getting tired of it too," says Rodney. "So let's eat."

"Hmm, ham and cheese with lettuce and tomato. You did a good job Rodney," exclaims Renee after a bite of her sandwich.

"After we eat, we're going on a little road trip to see an old friend. You will have to come along until the spell wears off. You understand that when anyone else is around, you will still act like a four-year-old, have a problem with your walking and left arm, as well as your speech difficulties?" I ask just to make sure he doesn't break out too soon. We may still have a chance at the potion when we see Joe.

After lunch, we go down to the VW and I make Rodney get in the back seat. He's a bit too tall but can sit with his legs on the other side of the car. I go straight east to pick up 24th Ave East and turn north. We don't get too far until we hit a backup from the Montlake Bridge which appears to be stuck open. Once the bridge closes and we get across, I take Montlake Boulevard, swing onto 45th and keep on going as it turns into Sand Point Way. I drive past the Laurelhurst area then east on 70th. I weave around a bit until we arrive at Joe's house at the end of 41st Avenue off 80th.

There are three cars parked in the end of the street so I don't have a choice and park in his driveway. I get out and push the seat forward for Rodney to get out while Renee gets out too.

"You stay right here, Rodney and don't go anywhere. Understand?"

"Y-ess, Mr. D-arryl-l," he says apparently aware someone could overhear us.

Renee and I go up to the door and ring the bell. We wait a minute or so, the door cracks open against a chain and a woman's voice asks, "Who's there?"

"Uh, it's Darryl and Renee. Is Joe home?" I ask.

"No one name Joe lives here," comes the answer.

"Excuse me, Ma'am, but I've visited Joe at this house many times. Are you sure Joe's not here?"

An eyeball looks through the crack in the door and answers, "I've lived here for almost 40 years and there's no one on this block named Joe." The door slams and locks.

I stare at Renee and she stares back. I slowly turn and walk back to the car. She doesn't say a word but just walks along beside me.

"You guys see a ghost?" asks Rodney as we approach the car.

"Get in and shut up," I snap. I'm in no mood to deal with him.

I don't say anything on our trip back to Rodney's house. I'm trying to understand what is going on. How could I have known Joe for several years and come to this very house regularly and now have someone else living there? How could his New Age Apothecary suddenly turn into a bookstore?

When we get back inside, I tell Rodney to go to his room and wait for us to get him. I head for the kitchen for a beer. Renee trails along behind me. She's being unusually quiet.

I grab a bottle from the frig and pop the top off with the bottle opener attached to the counter by the frig. I hand it to Renee and grab another for myself. I sit down on the bench behind the breakfast nook by the window overlooking the side yard and the neighbor's house. Renee pulls up a chair near me and stares at me. I stare back. Neither of us touches our beers.

Finally, I speak, "I guess we're going to have to let the spell wear off or let him out of it on command, take our $500 and get out of here."

"You know, after hearing about this Voice yesterday, then having Joe vanish, I would like some answers. Don't you give a rat's behind about what happened?" I can see that Renee is starting to boil inside.

"Yeah, I care. But it's beyond me. Don't you remember; I started out taking engineering classes? I'm all logical and that kind of stuff; this doesn't make one bit of sense and doesn't fit into anything that I can explain or understand. It's just too Twilight Zone for me. I'm scared!" OK, I admit it. I didn't want to say that but I did.

"Well, at least it helps to know that you're scared too." Renee softens for a moment then her anger returns as she slams her hand on the table. I jump. "What about that Voice, why doesn't he tell you something? Where is that S.O.B?"

"I don't know; he only talks to me when he wants. I don't have any control over him. It certainly would be a good time to get some direction from him." I look around the ceiling of the room with my hands up. "Huh, how about it? Would you like to tell us what's going on?"

Nothing – I get nothing. I'm frustrated and starting to get a bit angry myself.

Renee sits back in her chair shaking her head. "I guess you're right. Let's cut Rodney loose and get out of here." She leans forward again. "But I'm telling you, if there is any more of this Voice stuff happening, I'm not sticking around. Right now, I'm not even sure if I'm sticking around Voice or no Voice."

"What are you saying?"

"What does it sound like? I'm on the verge of leaving you and this life on the edge of poverty not knowing if we'll score enough to make the next rent payment and eating crap to make ends meet." She stands up and turns away from me, crossing her arms.

I get up and take hold of her shoulders. "Honey, I had no idea you were feeling this way. I thought you liked the excitement of the scams and that having little just kept us from being like all the money grubbing yuppies."

She turns and pulls away. "Excitement, yes, but it isn't compensating for scraping by. Now you add this Voice thing to it and I'm not sure I want to be around you."

"But, doesn't the way we make love mean anything?" I know what she really likes.

"Don't flatter yourself, Darryl. I can find plenty of horny guys any time I want," she responds with a sneer.

Oh that hurts. Maybe I don't know her as well as I thought. "No, Renee, you have to hang in here. I know we can work this out. I don't want to lose you."

"Yeah, I know what you don't want to lose, sex," she snaps back.

OK, that doesn't just hurt, it makes me mad. I take a menacing step toward Renee and she backs up against the counter in the middle of the kitchen. Before I realize what's happening, she grabs a butcher knife from the knife block and waves it in front of me.

"Take one more step and you're going to regret it!" she screams.

I freeze. I back up and raise my hands in surrender. "Hold on, what's going on? We never fight like this."

"It's the damn Voice, Darryl. It's gotta be that insane spiritual thing," she's still yelling.

"No, it can't be. The Voice has never steered me wrong. There's something else going on here. Let's just try to calm down and see how it plays out." I go back and sit down at the nook.

Renee slowly puts the knife back but stays by the counter. I wait without saying anything. I'm determined not to react like that again. Finally, she says, "OK, so what's the plan?"

"Let's get Rodney back to himself, get our money, and see where we go from there. We need to talk and find out what we really want to be doing with our lives." I can't think of anything else to say, no thanks to The Voice.

Renee takes a deep breath, "OK, but we take it one step at a time."

"OK, I'll get Rodney." I get up and go to his bedroom.

I knock on his door and tell him to come downstairs.

"Oh-kay, Mr. D-darryl," he responds.

I head back down the stairs and hear his door open and then hear him following me, dragging his foot on the carpet.

I tell him to sit on the couch. Renee is standing at the kitchen door watching. "Rodney, when I count to three and snap my fingers, you will return to normal. You will vaguely remember your medical exam but nothing else that has occurred since you came under the spell. Do you understand?"

"Y-yes, Mr. D-darryl," he answers.

I wonder why he is stammering but really don't care. I look at Renee to make sure she's on board. She nods her head. "One, two, three." I snap my fingers.

"So, Rodney, you should be getting your 4-F designation in couple of weeks." I realize that without Joe, we won't be able to do a follow up. I almost told him that he could contact us if they require another exam. This could turn bad if they do. "So, if you'll give us the remaining $500, we'll be on our way."

"Oh-kay, Mr. D-darryl," says Rodney as he gets up and hobbles to his office. I follow far enough so I can watch as he opens a drawer in the desk and removes an envelope. He hobbles back and hands me the envelope. "D-do you h-ave to g-go, Mr. D-darryl?" he asks.

"Uh, Rodney, you don't have to talk that way or walk like that. No one is here to see or hear you except Renee and me," I say as I take the envelope. I don't look up but check to make sure the money is there. Yup, five crisp C notes. I look at Renee and nod.

"Thanks for the business, Rodney, we'll be going now. The best of luck to you," says Renee as we walk toward the door.

Rodney starts whimpering and we stop and turn around.

"B-but wh-oo will ta-ke c-are of me?" asks Rodney.

"Rodney, snap out of it. You are no longer under the spell. You can walk without any problems, you don't have to talk or act like a four-year-old and you can use your left arm and hand just like you used to be able to do," I say sternly.

You want to bet about that? The Voice says to me.

Now Rodney is really crying. He isn't faking it; he is just like a four-year-old.

"Aw, don't worry, Rodney, we'll take care of you. We'll take real good care of you. We won't leave you after all." I smile at Renee and point to my head. Her eyes get big and as she raises her eyebrows.

Rodney jumps up and down and claps his hands saying thank you over and over. I calm him down and send him back to his room so I can talk to Renee.

After he leaves, she says, "The Voice spoke to you again?"

"Yes, it appears that this spell is quite different than the previous ones. I think this may be a permanent condition for Rodney."

"You think? It appears? Do you know for sure?" she asks.

I bite my lip. "No I don't know for sure, but we said we'd take it one step at a time and look where this step to take him out of the spell took us, exactly where we want to be. Rodney is obviously still messed up and now we have the means to clean him out or whatever we want to do," I try to sound convincing.

"You don't sound all that sure, Darryl. What happens if he suddenly wakes up?"

One step at a time, says The Voice.

"The Voice says we need to take one step at a time. I think we have to demonstrate some faith in his guidance. He must be the reason Rodney didn't wake up." I don't have to sound convinced now; I am convinced.

"What does this mean?" she asks.

"It means, that one of us will need to go back home and get some of our stuff because we're going to be living here for a while." I gesture toward the beautifully decorated living room, then the big kitchen, then with a huge smile, Rodney's office. "Isn't this what you wanted?"

"Ah, yes, I do believe I could get used to this house," nods Renee.

Chapter Seven

I sit Rodney down to watch some TV while Renee and I go into his office to find out what we can do to manage his affairs. The first thing to do is find out how much cash he has in the safe. Renee pulls the copy of "The Potato Eaters" to the side, revealing the safe. She is good with numbers and doesn't even have to look up the combination.

I'm really impressed by the quality of his safe, not to mention the copy of the Van Gogh. This isn't just a thin stick-it-between two studs cheapo wall safe. The interior is twelve inches deep, fourteen wide, and sixteen inches high. It has several drawers and several legal sized folders on shelves.

Renee gasps as she opens one of the small envelope sized drawers, "Darryl, look at this!"

I look over her shoulder as she's moving her fingers back and forth counting some good sized diamonds. "Whoa, what's he doing with this many diamonds?"

"I don't know, but this one drawer must be worth a quarter of a million. There's 30 big ones in here. Do you think he'd miss one?" she asks.

"Not in his current state. Does he have a list anywhere that someone might be able to inventory them against? We'll also need to look for insurance policies." I pull one of the folders out to see what's so important that he keeps it in a safe with a bunch of diamonds. It's a pretty thick folder.

I browse through a bunch of legal documents, a will, and two death certificates. They are what Renee found before showing how Rodney got all his money. It looks like his parents were killed in a plane crash while flying to Yakima from Seattle. Wow, he inherited the whole shebang without any strings attached. I laugh, "I wonder if Rodney even knows how much he has."

I look at Renee to see if she's even listening. I can see why if she hasn't. She's counting $100 bills. "Did you hear me?" I ask.

"What?" she snaps, "Dang, you made me lose count." She gives me a dirty look and says, "Yes, I heard. You wonder if he even knows how much he has. He's filthy rich because his parents left him everything. That's all I need to know."

"How much is there?" I ask.

"Now, who's not listening? I said I lost count," she says as she waves a fist full of money in front of my face. "Let's see, I've got seven piles of ten each, and that's about half, so I'm guessing around $14,000 just in the safe."

"Well, that should last a while for incidental expenses," I joke, "until we can get control of the rest. That could be more money than I've made in my life."

"Yeah, me too. I can't imagine having this much money just lying around in the house. Why isn't it in a bank getting interest or invested in the stock market? Is he just crazy?" says Renee, then continues counting.

I keep on looking through the safe. The manila envelope he had yesterday is in there so I take it out. It's still sealed. I wonder why it's so important that he put it in the safe, but didn't open it. There aren't any stamps on it so it was hand delivered. I open it. Inside is a folder; in the folder is a mug shot of a young woman, not flattering at all. There's also a rap sheet for an Elizabeth Wesley to match the number on the picture. Along with it is a report by a PI and three photographs of the same woman with three different guys.

"Hey, Renee, does she look familiar to you? I think I've seen her somewhere before." I hold up the mug shot.

Renee takes a quick glance then pulls another folder out of the file cabinet. She's finished looking though the safe. "Yeah, that's Sydney, Rodney's fiancée."

"What? No way. Sydney was way –" I stop before I get in trouble.

"Gorgeous? Yeah, you're a guy and that's why you didn't recognize the mug shot," says Renee as she turns a smug look at me, one hand on her hip. "And you are in trouble. So what's the deal on her?"

"Well," I take a close look at the rap sheet and the PI report. "Yeah, looks like she has a habit of getting engaged to rich guys, getting a big rock and other gifts then disappears. One time she got on a joint banking account before the wedding, then took off with everything. PI traced down a whole bunch more incidents than the cops did. Probably because the embarrassed to-be didn't want to say anything."

"Pretty slick, we'd better watch out if she comes back. That little fight wasn't nearly bad enough for him to have confronted her with this evidence. Maybe she was here when the PI delivered the envelope. Oh, I better check to see if they have a joint account." Renee starts digging through the file cabinet. "Here, check this one out," she says as she hands me a folder and keeps on thumbing through the files.

I take a look and sit down at the desk. It has a year's worth of statements from Walston & Company, a stock brokerage. "This guy has quite a portfolio. The bottom line on these statements is three million plus."

"After looking at all he has here, I'm not surprised," says Renee as she looks up. "I'm finding folders on different real estate holdings. From the looks of this, he must be clearing over fifty grand a month in rent from office buildings and apartment buildings."

"No wonder he wanted to avoid the draft," I answer as I shake my head. I have a hard time imagining anyone having all this. I sit down at the desk to peruse the statements some more and comment, "You know, there has been an awful lot of trading going on in these accounts. I wouldn't have thought he had time to do this, go to school, and party too."

"Oh crap!" exclaims Renee as she pulls out a thick folder.

"What's wrong?" I ask.

"He's got an attorney. Why didn't we think of this before? If we try to make a move on any of these accounts, we may end up in deep trouble," she says as she slams the folder down on the desk in front of me.

I look in the folder and find a Power of Attorney and other documents giving his attorney authority to handle all his holdings. "It looks like he really trusts this guy, Renee. It looks like the attorney gives him an allowance each month and apart from that Rodney doesn't have to worry about anything. The attorney does it all."

"That does it. Maybe we should just take as much as can't be traced or raise suspicion and clear out. Let the attorney worry about taking care of Rodney if he doesn't wake up." Dejection is all over Renee's voice.

The Voice says, *Dig deeper*.

"Not yet, Renee. There may be more here than meets the eye. The Voice wants us to keep going and see what we can turn up. Maybe there's something the attorney doesn't know about or doesn't control," I answer as I keep looking through the folder.

Rodney interrupts us by telling us he's hungry again. I tell him to go and make us all a nice dinner. He cheerfully says OK and shuffles off to the kitchen. I don't think about it anymore until I hear a pan crash on the kitchen floor and Rodney scream.

I race to the kitchen to see the gas range turned on and Rodney shaking his hand and crying. There is a pan of half-cooked macaroni splattered all over the floor. "Good grief, Rodney, what happened?" I ask.

"I-I bu-urned m-my h-hand."

"Let me see." I grab his hand; fortunately there isn't any blistering so I run some cold water and have him hold his hand in it. Renee grabs a dustpan and scoops up the macaroni and puts it in the garbage. There's a mop in the closet and I use it to clean up the water.

I pick up the pan by the handle and it's still quite hot so I use a hot pad. The handle shouldn't be that hot. I look at the stove and see two burners on. I'll bet he had the handle too close to the second burner. What a bummer. I was hoping he would still be able to do things like he did when he fixed lunch.

"Go back in to the TV room and watch some more. I'll make dinner," says Renee with a sigh.

Rodney leaves and I look at Renee, shaking my head. "This might not be as easy as I thought it would be. I think we have a 180-pound four-year-old on our hands. At least he's still being obedient. I don't know what I'd do if he weren't."

I go back to the office and start pouring over all the file folders. After dinner Renee joins me and we continue to assess Rodney's financial and legal position.

The evening passes quickly and we put Rodney to bed then crash ourselves. I'm tired and still quite anxious about our situation so I don't sleep all that well.

The next morning at 5:30, we are awakened by Rodney banging on our door. "I'll bet he slept like a baby," I groan.

"Yeah," agrees Renee. "You get to make sure he showers and gets dressed. I'm not taking care of that big hulk."

I open the door and lead Rodney back to his room. I get him in the shower and stick close by to make sure he doesn't do something rash. I also peruse his medicine cabinet. Darn, he uses a safety razor. Why would a rich kid do that? I don't want him getting close to it or he's liable to end up with cuts all over his face. Note to self to buy an electric, or maybe we can just let him grow a beard.

I don't suggest that he shave today and he doesn't even seem to think about it. After he is dressed, I send him downstairs to wait for Renee and me – without doing any cooking. I return to our guest room and shower since Renee is dressed and ready to go downstairs too.

"Keep an eye on Rodney, I don't know what he might be up to at this time of day," I warn Renee.

"Well, all he's getting from me this morning is cold cereal and a cup of coffee," she replies.

"Coffee for a four-year," I start, then think about what I was about to say. "Yeah, I'll be down shortly."

After breakfast Renee takes Rodney for a walk while I continue to look through the records. Renee is gone about a half hour when the front door opens. I call out, "You back already?"

"Who is that?" comes back the reply. "Is that you, Mr. McNairy?" The voice has a foreign accent.

I leave the office and see a short, dark woman standing in the entryway with a set of keys in her hand. I size her up, medium dark black hair with hint of grey in places. She's wearing denim jeans and a short brown jacket. My guess is the housecleaner.

"Who are you?" She challenges with more authority than I expected.

"I'm Mr. McNairy's financial advisor, Darryl Smith," I respond. "And you are Mrs. Rosie Rodriquez, I expect." I'm making a guess, but I did see the name on a pay record.

"Uh, si, how did you know my name and since when did Mr. McNairy have a financial advisor?" She isn't letting up.

"As I said, I'm his advisor and I've been going over his financial statements and I've seen that he has paid you regularly. I'm not sure why yet, but I'm guessing you are the one who cleans up after him. Is that right?" I ask.

"Si, but I've never seen you before."

"Well, Mr. McNairy has developed a serious malady and as long as he was capable of tending to his own affairs, I was only on a retainer." I stop and shake my head. "But now, it looks like you'll be seeing a lot of me as I'll be paying you. Perhaps you could help me by letting me know what your arrangements were. By the way, you can call me Darryl."

Next, I have to explain to Rosie about Rodney, that he's out for a walk with Renee and will be back soon and she can see for herself his condition. For a housecleaner, she is pretty sharp. Finally, she's satisfied that I'm not some thief who has just broken in. Yeah, I'm a thief who has been here two days. I get to go back to examining the books and she goes to work cleaning.

During the morning the phone rings several times. I ignore it and some people leave messages. Mostly people who are his friends, mostly friends who want to borrow some money. I wonder how we are going to deal with all these people.

Renee returns with Rodney after an hour and a half. Rodney is loaded down with bags from the neighborhood Bartell Drug store.

"You couldn't have walked all the way down to Bartell's from here," I say. "What is all of this and where did you get the cash for it?" I ask.

"From the safe, silly," she answers, "on our walk, I asked Rodney what he liked to do and I realized that he doesn't have any toys, so we came back and took the car down. I figured that he would get bored watching TV all the time so here we are."

"Wow, smart lady. What do you say about having kids of your own?"

Renee gives me a dirty look, "I think this is as close as I want to come." She points to Rodney.

I fill Renee in on Rosie, and then she takes off to find her.

I take Rodney downstairs to the rec room with his toys. Once he is absorbed in opening packages, I leave him and go back to the office.

A short while later, Renee comes in looking all happy, even gloating.

"So what's got you in such a good mood?" I ask.

"You know that taking care of Rodney is going to be a bigger chore that I ever imagined so I talked to Rosie. I took her downstairs and Rodney didn't even recognize her. After our chat, I found out she has a lot of connections with people who can do all the dirty work while we do the financials. I don't think they will ask a lot of questions as long as we pay them well."

"That sounds super to me. When you first mentioned keeping him in this state it sounded like a great idea. Now, after less than a day of taking care of him, I was about to go along with your suggestion to cut and run regardless of what The Voice says. But this may be the way to go." I'm feeling a lot better about the whole situation. "When will they be able to help?" I ask.

"I've got it covered. We'll have babysitting starting this afternoon. Rosie is going to make sure we have someone to stay overnight, keep him occupied, do grocery shopping, and anything else we want," she says as she sits in my lap and gives me a hug. "We are going to be on easy street, my Sweet!"

"Well I hope you're right. I'd hate to have so much done for us that we don't have any cash left for ourselves. Not only that but I still have to figure out how to deal with that lawyer." I'm not quite sold yet, but it certainly feels better than it did.

"Oh, stop being a party pooper. Your Voice will surely help us out," says Renee as she starts to kiss me.

OK, I can take a break and let this go wherever she wants.

Later, I come back to the office and continue through the books. Then it hits me. All that trading going on in Rodney's stock account, there's something odd about that. I've heard of brokers churning customers' accounts to earn the brokerage fees so I take another look. According to the statements, the activity isn't the broker buying and selling, but transfers in and out with cash settlements for the transfers. The value of the stock at the transfer time isn't listed.

Dang, I wish I had an easy way to find out the historical prices of the stocks that are being moved. Right now all I have is Rodney's statements. Some of the statements have the values at the end of the previous month, but some of the transfers are done both in and out during the month so I can't get the actual value.

I find a slide rule in Rodney's desk and start listing the ones with values and the cash amounts that appear to be related to the transfers. I calculate the amount paid for the transfer in or the amount received after a transfer out for the ones I can calculate. I then list the last known value of the stock in a previous statement.

I check out ten of the stocks this way and discover that the transfers out received significantly less cash than the value of the stock. The transfers in cost significantly more than the value of the stock in the next month's statement.

So that's it. Rodney's attorney is transferring stock in and getting a lot more for the stock than it is worth. When he moves it out, probably to his own account, he is paying much less than the stock is worth. He is slowly but methodically draining Rodney's account, all the while not taking risk in the market himself.

With this dirt on the lawyer, there is no way he'll challenge our taking over his Power of Attorney. All I need to do is to get more details from Walston & Company. I can't wait to tell Renee so I take off to find out what she's up to.

Chapter Eight

Right after breakfast, Felipe, Rosie's cousin, takes care of Rodney. Thanks to Rosie's team, I'm free to call up Walston & Company. I tell them that I've got a new Power of Attorney to file with them for Rodney's account and I'll be over in a half hour. The guy on the other end of the phone sounds stilted as he says he'll look up the account number and puts me on hold. When he returns he practically falls all over himself being nice. I guess he doesn't handle too many multi-million dollar accounts.

Renee brought over some more of our clothes yesterday so I get dressed in a suit. Yuk, I hope I don't have to do this too often.

Renee also dresses up with a conservative business type outfit. She puts her hair up in a bun and gets some really nerdy dark rimmed glasses. I think she could pass for a lawyer or paralegal without any problem.

We then go to the Walston & Company's office downtown Seattle in the NB of C building. Pretty ritzy place and quite new; it speaks of money from the bottom to the top. We take the elevator to the 40th floor and enter the brokerage through huge glass doors. Ticker tapes and green computer screens are both being used to display stock prices. Several people are standing around looking at them and some taking notes. I walk up to the receptionist and ask for Clarence Sutherland, Rodney's broker. She picks up the phone and tells Clarence we're here.

Clarence comes out of a door to the receptionist's left and introduces himself. I in turn introduce Renee as my legal beagle and he ushers us to a corner office with glass walls. OK, maybe he has several multi-million dollar accounts and he just knows how to be nice to them. We sit down in some very nice leather chairs around a glass coffee table near his desk.

"So, Mr. Smith, I understand that you have a new Power of Attorney that supersedes Mr. McNairy's current one that is on file with us?" asks Clarence very nicely but with authority.

"That's correct, Mr. Sutherland. Miss Cleve, will you provide the documents for Mr. Sutherland?" I ask of Renee.

As Renee opens her briefcase, Clarence comments, "We called Mr. McNairy's attorney after you called and he indicated he had not been informed that Mr. McNairy had made a new Power of Attorney." He leans over and takes the Power of Attorney from Renee and starts to read it.

I really didn't want to clue Mr. Trickey into the fact that we were kicking him out until we had more evidence. Oh well, the cat's out of the bag. I just hope Clarence doesn't question our documents.

"I didn't want to inform Mr. Trickey of the changes until I'd come to you," I stall because I'm not sure if I should spill the beans that Trickey has been systematically cleaning out Rodney's account. So I just wait as Clarence looks over the document.

"Well, it seems that these documents are in order, but I'm surprised that they're dated only this weekend. I may have to have our legal look them over before we allow you access to the account," states Clarence.

Renee jumps in, "Mr. Sutherland, these are legal documents and I'm familiar enough with procedures in brokerage houses to know that you don't need to have anyone else review them."

Wow, I love the way she is able to make someone squirm, and Clarence is. Now it's my turn, "Mr. Sutherland, because of the anomalies we've found in Mr. McNairy's statements, we are not only requesting to have full access to his account, but we are going to need to find out exactly where the following transfers have come from or gone to." I take out the stack of statements from the briefcase and show him the ones with transfers that I circled.

"I don't know if I can do that. This is quite an unusual request," replies Clarence.

I smile and stand up as I say, "Very well, Mr. Sutherland, it appears that you have reason to be uncooperative. I want you to get your superior in here on the double or we are going to the feds and the SEC."

"Uh, no, wait. I can get that information for you," backpedals Clarence.

"Too late, Mr. Sutherland," says Renee, "you had your chance to prove that you had nothing to do with these anomalies."

She sits back in her chair as I stare down Clarence as The Voice has told me. I watch as beads of sweat break out on Clarence's forehead. He slowly gets up and goes to his desk, then dials someone on his phone. I can't hear what he says but he turns away from us and talks much longer than I would have expected. He finally hangs up and comes back and stands behind his chair.

"Mr. Bigelow, the branch manager, will be here in a couple of minutes," says Clarence weakly. "I have my secretary pulling the information you requested."

Now I think that's pretty unusual since he didn't take the transaction information I had asked about to the phone with him. The Voice tells me to ask him some questions.

"So, Mr. Sutherland, how long have you been helping Mr. Trickey skim off the account?"

Clarence takes a deep breath and answers, "Trickey came to me shortly after McNairy established his account with us. He knew I owed a lot of money on my gambling debts. It was either hook up with him or face the ire of my creditors."

"How did he know you owed for gambling?" I ask. The Voice assures me that as keep eye contact, he will spill the beans.

"Trickey seems well connected with them. When I initially refused, I was visited that night by some goons who made it clear that my debts would be paid one way or another if I didn't cooperate with Trickey. Of course, they didn't implicate him directly." Clarence isn't looking good and is shaking. He sits down only to get up quickly as an older man in a very expensive suit enters the room followed by a young woman holding a ream of papers.

"I'm a busy man, Clarence; what's going on?" The man looks at Clarence, then at Renee and me.

Clarence starts, "Mr. Bigelow, this is Mr. Smith and Miss Cleve. They have presented documentation showing that they now represent Mr.

McNairy, one of my largest accounts –" Clarence appears to run out of gas.

I speak up, "Mr. Bigelow, Clarence has just admitted to us that he and Mr. McNairy's previous attorney have been skimming off my client's account. I believe the young lady behind you has the documentation that will prove this."

"Holy cow, Clarence, is this true?" bellows Bigelow.

"Yes, Sir, it's true," says Clarence as he hangs his head.

Bigelow turns to the young lady. "Maggie, put those on Clarence's desk then you can leave us."

Maggie puts them on the desk and exits the room quickly. I watch her out of the corner of my eye and can see her stop at the desk of what appears to be the secretary of another broker. Two more ladies immediately come to the desk and they start talking. News travels fast here.

Bigelow is now thumbing through the papers that were deposited on Clarence's desk. A lot of uh-huhs are emanating from him as he looks at the papers. After a couple of minutes, he turns back to us.

"I'm so sorry that this unfortunate lapse of integrity has occurred at our branch. It appears that these transfers are all going to the same account. It appears, Mr. Smith, that you are correct. Mr. Trickey has been plundering his client's account. We want to do everything we can to rectify this. If you will leave the Power of Attorney with me, I'll make the necessary arrangements and have the account status changed to show you have full access. In addition I will assign a new broker to work with you," says Bigelow as he smacks his lips and feigns disgust.

I'm pretty sure that Bigelow is in on this just as deep as Clarence because he knows that Trickey is the one who had control of the account. I step over to the desk and look at the same papers that he just thumbed through. Sure enough, there are only account numbers on the transfers, no names. Not only that, if we leave the original of the Power of Attorney with him, there will be no evidence that we are able to have access to the account.

"Mr. Bigelow, since this is a grave criminal act that has occurred in your branch, I wouldn't keep any of Mr. McNairy's assets here even if the president of the company assured me that they would be safe. So, unless you want me to call the FBI, you will immediately prepare me bearer certificates for all of Mr. McNairy's stocks and bonds. You will provide a cashier's check for all cash in the account and we will wait right here while you do that. In addition, I will be taking this documentation with me." I pick up the stack that Maggie put on Clarence's desk.

Bigelow starts to protest and The Voice assures me that the evil eye will work on him, so I stare him down and he leaves in a huff.

"Wow, that was quite a move, Darryl," says Renee. "What's up?"

"I think we and Rodney are in danger. We need to get those certificates and clear out as quickly as possible. Keep an eye on the door; I need to warn Rosie." I quickly use Clarence's phone to call Rosie. I look out the window at the magnificent view of Puget Sound and the Olympic Mountains beyond. I have the strange feeling that I've been here before.

I tell Rosie that she needs to pack a bag for Rodney, clean out his safe and get the files I had left on his desk. I tell her to meet us at a coffee shop near our apartment and not to tell anyone except her cousin who is on duty with Rodney. "And do it as quickly as you can!" I add as I hang up.

Bigelow returns soon afterward with a briefcase. I go over the bearer certificates to make sure they match everything on Rodney's account. Fortunately there are no discrepancies. I thank Bigelow and we quickly exit to the lobby.

We get into an elevator and I push the lowest floor that is above the transition point where the elevators don't stop for the lower floors of the building. When it stops, we get out and go around the corner to the elevator lobby for the lower floors. We catch one and I punch the second floor. When we get there, we exit and take the stairs. I'm betting that there will be a welcoming committee waiting at the high-rise elevators for us.

At the door to the lobby I motion to Renee to be quiet as I slowly open the door a crack and look into the elevator lobby. I let the door close after my peek.

"Darn, I can spot two goons trying to be nonchalant near the revolving doors. They have a good view of both elevator lobbies."

"What are we going to do?" asks Renee. "The elevators don't go to the parking garage and this is the end of the stairs. Crap, they probably have the garage covered, too."

"Right now, I'm not sure. We could go back up and try to find a place to hide but I'm afraid they won't leave until we do." I'm wondering if we took off a bigger bite than we can chew when The Voice says to look again.

I look out the door and the goons are on the move. "Come on," I whisper to Renee and we walk slowly into the lobby and look around the corner. The goons are following a couple that is dressed exactly like us! If I didn't know better, I would say they were us, even carrying a briefcase just like ours and the one Bigelow gave us for the certificates.

We follow at a distance as they exit the building through the revolving doors with the goons at a respectable distance. They aren't going to try anything in the building. I check to make sure that there aren't any other obvious lookouts and we slip through the doors.

Once outside I look up the street to where the bug is parked and the couple is heading straight for it. Renee tugs on my sleeve and we turn to walk the other way. We slip around the building and then turn back to see what's happening.

The couple crosses the street and goes to our car and they get in. What is going on, who are they? The goons aren't following, they are just watching from this side of the street. Suddenly the car explodes; there is metal and burning debris flying all over the street. The blast, even though a block away, almost deafens me. People are running in all directions, some toward the car and others away. The two goons just continue on our side of the street and disappear around the corner.

"What just happened?" asks Renee.

I put my arm around her and we start walking to our next destination, the Merrill Lynch office. "I think we were just blown up by Trickey's mob." Renee is shaking. "We'll be safe. The Voice told me just in time to walk out when the goons left. I think that somehow, he put those two in our car and made it look like us. Trickey won't be looking for us for a while and we have time to unload these certificates and find a safe place for us."

"Whew, I sure hope you're right. I never thought we'd end up playing with the big boys," says Renee as she calms down a bit. "These guys are playing for keeps."

Within five minutes we're in the Merrill Lynch office and present the certificates to them. We set up the account in Rodney's name and explain why we're moving everything – except the goons and our car being blown up. No use bringing that up. Fortunately, we have a post office box that we use for the address on the account. I don't trust using Rodney's home address.

Our next stop is the National Bank of Commerce. Since I hadn't seen anything wrong with Rodney's bank statements, my only concern is to move the money so that Trickey can't get his hands on it. I stop at a teller and let her know that I need to speak with the manager.

An older man dressed in a nice pinstriped suit including a vest immediately invites us into his office. I chuckle in my mind as I watch the stately man lead us to his office. If he says his name is Mr. Banks, I'm going to ask if he knows where Mary Poppins went. His name isn't Banks, it's Smith so he must be one of my long lost relatives.

I explain that I have just acquired the Power of Attorney over Rodney's assets and wish to move them to another bank. Smith simply nods and looks over the documents that Renee produces from her briefcase. He presses a button on his phone and tells the lady on the other end to come to his office.

An older lady, slim and dressed in a suit quickly comes to the door. I'm thinking Miss Hathaway but Smith asks Mrs. Burk to close the account and issue us a cashier's check. Ten minutes later, we are on the way to Seattle-First National Bank to set up a new account, less two grand for our upcoming expenses.

After we leave Seattle-First, we grab a cab and go back to meet up with Rosie and Rodney.

Chapter Nine

We arrive at the coffee shop just after 1:00 pm. I'm famished and looking to get something to eat and find some time to relax. This has been an exhausting morning. We enter and look around. Fortunately, we see Rosie, Rodney, and her cousin at a booth near the back. Renee slides in next to Rosie and I grab a chair to sit at the end of the booth. Rodney is hemmed in on the inside by Rosie's cousin. I take one look at Rosie and see one very concerned lady. Renee doesn't look all that relaxed either.

"How did it go, Rosie? Were you able to get the stuff we wanted?" I ask, trying to be calm and in control.

"Si, Darryl, we were able to open the safe and get the files you wanted," says Rosie as she shakes her head. "We called a cab and left the house out the back and met it around the block, just as you asked. We were a few blocks away when we heard a very loud explosion. I asked the cab driver to go back. When we got close to the house, there was a huge fire and parts of the house were in the street. We immediately turned around and came straight here." Rosie starts to tremble as she finishes. "What is going on?"

"Oh my …" exclaims Renee as she covers her mouth. "What is going on is right! They blow up our car then they blow up Rodney's house; what's next?"

"House went ka-boom," says Rodney as he puts his hands together then quickly opens them like an explosion.

"Who are they?" asks Rosie.

"'They' happens to be Rodney's old attorney, Mr. Trickey. He just happened to be skimming assets out of Rodney's account. He is apparently closely connected with people who like to blow things up. I have a feeling that if we continue to look at Rodney's previous arrangement with Trickey, we'll find that he has total control of Rodney's estate should Rodney die," I explain.

Felipe lets out a quiet whistle, "Do you need some protection? I know some guys that would be willing to keep an eye out for those thugs."

I'm stunned and hesitate before answering, "What are you talking about? We have enough on those guys to call the cops and put them away. I don't think I want to get into a mob war."

Felipe smiles craftily, "Hey, I'm not some dumb babysitter. I can put two and two together. Last week, Rodney is just a party animal who's scared of the draft. This week, he's a four-year-old living in a 20-something body. The word on the street is that there's a couple who can get you past the draft by faking a head injury that makes you act like a four-year-old. Sound familiar?" asks Felipe.

I'm not hungry anymore. I look at Renee, she is maintaining a stoic face; she's really good at poker. But her touch under the table lets me know she's really concerned. "I'm listening," I say. This would be a good time for The Voice to inject something like do the evil eye thing but I'm getting nothing.

Felipe continues, "So I'm guessing something goes wrong with whatever it is that you do to get Rodney back to normal, or maybe you see how much he's worth and decide to ride it out as long as you can. Am I getting close, Darryl?"

I'm not going to give it up this quick, but he certainly has us pegged. "Keep going," I say matter-of-factly.

He sits back and smiles, "Amigo, you are in way over your head. Suddenly, a two-bit con artist and his girlfriend," Felipe glances at Renee, "find themselves face to face with the big boys. Guys who play for keeps and don't like losing out on millions. Si, I can read stock statements too. You want some help or not?"

He's right; we are in way over our heads. But, I'm not sure this is the way to go. "I need to think about this," I reply.

Felipe leans forward and says in a low voice, "Don't think too long. Either we help you or we let you go on your own. No help with Rodney, no help with the mob, and I'm pretty sure you aren't going to the cops or they will smell a rat just as easily as we did." He smiles at Rosie who winks back at him. "Oh, just remember that the cops are going to come looking for the owner of that car that blew up. What are you going to tell them?"

"Renee and I need to talk. We'll be back in a few minutes," I answer and stand up. Renee slides out of the booth.

As we start to head toward the front of the shop Rosie speaks up, "Don't be gone long. Remember, we have the diamonds for our trouble but we won't keep Rodney forever like you would."

We go outside where they can't hear or see us. Renee starts talking as soon as we get out the door, "I say we cut and run. We can get thousands in cash and disappear. This is all just too scary."

Before she can continue, I point across the street. I watch as an unmarked cop car pulls up to the loading zone in front of our apartment building. Two plainclothes cops get out and enter the building. "I'll bet they're looking for us regarding the car."

"There is just too much going on. He's right; what are we going to tell them?" asks Renee.

I tell Renee to stay put and I run across the street. I look in the door to make sure the cops aren't in sight and go in. I can hear them still on the stairs so I start up quietly; I'm glad the stairs are carpeted. The cops are pretty heavy footed as they trudge up to the third floor. I stay back but can hear and see them knocking on our door as I'm a little over half way between the second and third floor. They wait and I'm nervous. I don't want them to see me. They slip something under the door and I drop back to the second floor and head down the hall toward the back stairs.

The cops continue down and I continue up the back stairs and see what they left. I open the door and retrieve an envelope. Inside is a handwritten note saying that my car caught fire downtown and that I should contact them. They left a number. I go back downstairs and make sure they are gone, and then cross back to Renee. I hand her the note.

"Just great. It's as if Felipe knew this in advance," says Renee.

"I know you want to cut and run but The Voice pointed out Rodney and said this would be fruitful. I haven't heard anything from him all the time Felipe was talking. At the stockbroker's, I was assured that just staring those guys down would make them cave in and they did. Now, I get nothing when Felipe has the goods on us. I tell you, Rene, we need to stick it out. If Felipe is right, he may just be the protection that The Voice wants us to have. I'm feeling more confident after having time across the street to think," I assure Renee.

Renee visibly relaxes. "I guess you're right. Besides, Rodney is loaded. There's enough for all of us."

I give her a hug. "I'm feeling better too. Let's see how much protection is going to cost us."

We go back inside and I order us a couple of ham sandwiches before sitting down. I'm hungry again.

"You took long enough, Amigo," says Felipe, not looking happy that we took our time.

"Yeah, I did. Cops showed up at our apartment. I had to check that out." I stick out my hand to Felipe and say, "Let's talk business."

He grabs my hand with a big smile, "You won't regret this."

The Voice tells me to warn him.

I squint my eyes and stare directly into his eyes, "And you will regret it if you try anything unbecoming, Friend." I squeeze his hand firmly.

It has the usual affect on Felipe as he loosens his grip. I can see the fear in his eyes.

We discuss the financial arrangements and how we are going to take care of things going forward. Rosie is assigned the task of finding a safe living space for Rodney and goes to the pay phone by the restrooms. Felipe will get the word out on the street that we are under his protection. That will make Trickey's people think twice before trying any more attacks. But we still have to be careful because we can't change Rodney's will while he is in his current state. That means if he dies, Trickey gets it all.

Felipe goes to the pay phone next to make arrangements while we see what Rosie managed to get before she left the house. She did a lot better than I thought she would. She has his ledger with information from the management companies taking care of Rodney's properties. That's crucial since I'll have to have them send payments to a new location. I wonder if

Trickey will get the address from them to try to hunt down Rodney. There are so many scenarios that my head feels like it is spinning.

Felipe comes back from the phone, "There will be two cars coming in five minutes. One will be for Rosie and Rodney to go to the safe house. The other will be for the rest of us to do whatever you need. I'll be with you."

"Sounds good for now. I'm going to call the cops to find out what they want to know about the car. I'll be back in a minute," I say as I take my turn on the phone.

I call the number and wait.

"O'Shawn speaking," comes the voice from the phone.

"Is Detective Markus there?" I ask.

"Wait one minute."

I wait and wonder why it is so quiet on the other end. I'm not on hold but there isn't any police station sounds coming from the phone.

"Markus is on a case right now. Can the detective meet you at the corner of Roosevelt Way and 15th at 8:30 tonight?" asks O'Shawn.

I hang up. That's not right. He didn't even ask who I was and to meet by a park and reservoir after dark? I don't think so.

I look in the phone book and get the local precinct phone number and address. I call them and ask how to report a stolen car. Dang, I have to go to the precinct to do it. I thank them and go back to our booth.

Rosie and Rodney have already left. Felipe wants to know where we want to go.

"Yea, take us to the police station at 10049 College Way North," I answer.

"Are you serious?" asks Renee.

"Yes, it appears that someone stole our car from our parking place last night. I just went to get it and it wasn't there. It's too bad that the door locks don't work and that a '52 VW is so easy to hotwire," I answer.

Renee and Felipe both laugh and we head for the door.

"Oh, and those cops that visited us are dirty. They work for Trickey. The number they gave was a set up. It looks like we'll need to make arrangement to move.

Felipe is doing things in style; a limousine with tinted windows is waiting for us at the curb. "I hope this is in our agreed budget," I comment as I get in.

"It's just temporary. The tinted windows will make sure that you won't be seen if we go anywhere Trickey's guys are watching. After things settle down, we'll work out something cheaper. However, if those cops are on Trickey's payroll, then it means they know you weren't killed and still pose a threat to him. So we need to be careful," replies Felipe as we settle in the back.

When we get to the police station, we park out of sight of the station. I don't want them to see me drive up in a limo and report a junker VW stolen. I go inside by myself while Renee and Felipe wait in the car. A very grumpy looking older man is on the desk. He asks lots of questions but there's no mention that the car has been blown up or even found. He looks grumpy but is quite friendly. When I tell them where I usually park, he just laughs and says I should find a better place to park. I agree; there isn't going to be any more on-the-street or alley parking for me.

I give him my old address but tell him that I'm in the process of moving so he tells me to check back regularly until I can update my address and phone number on file. I'm not sure I'm going to do that. All I want to do is make sure the cops don't come after me to clean up the mess after the explosion.

I get back to the car and Felipe asks, "So where to now?"

"Let's go check out Rodney's house. We need to see if there is still anything there we can salvage," I answer.

When we arrive, the street is blocked off and there is still a fire engine out front. We circle around and park about a block away.

"I don't want to go and start asking questions in case Trickey's guys are watching," I say. "How about you go and pose as working for the yard maintenance company Rodney uses?"

Felipe laughs and hands me a card as he gets out of the car. I look at the card and it is for a yard maintenance company. Right, what was I thinking? I suspect he has several different business cards.

"Where are we going to hole up tonight?" asks Renee. She's been pretty quiet lately.

"Let's get a hotel. I don't want to be around Rodney right now. Besides, if they find out where he is that could lead them to us or we could be conveniently taken care of at the same time." I shouldn't have said that last part. Renee brightened up at the mention of a hotel but grimaced that we could be harmed. "So where would you like to go?"

"Hmm, there's a very elegant older hotel in Seattle, the Sorrento. I've always wanted to stay there but it's always been out of my reach," says Renee.

"The Sorrento it is then. We'll go there next and settle in. I'm going to have to make some phone calls and that will be a good place to do it," I agree.

Felipe returns to the car and gets in.

"So what's it look like?" I ask.

"It looks like a burnt out hole in the ground. The fireman I talked to said that it looks like a gas leak in the basement ripped right through to the roof and set everything on fire that wasn't blown clear. There isn't anything left. He said any papers in the office outside of the safe would have been scattered and on fire. The filing cabinets were not fireproof so they are toast along with the contents. They found the safe but the door was open so they suppose it was blown open by the blast or when it came down. It's really a good thing you called Rosie or they would be looking for body parts right now," explained Felipe.

"Did they ask about Rodney?"

"Si, they did. I explained that Rosie had gone out with him shortly before and that no one should have been at home at the time. I explained as much as I could with my 'limited Mexican background,'" he uses air quotes, "that Rodney was incapacitated and Rosie took him to a relative. That means they're going to want to talk to you." Felipe hands me a card for the Captain.

"Great, just what I need, more phone calls and explanations."

Felipe slaps me on the back, "Hey, buck up. You wanted all this responsibility, didn't you? Oh, that's right; you just wanted the money." He laughs but I don't.

Chapter Ten

The limo pulls into the driveway of the Sorrento and stops under a green awning in front of the entrance. There's a fountain with water running down over three little nude cherubs on our left. Already I can see why Renee likes this place. Felipe gets out first and looks around, then holds the door open for us.

"Still doesn't look like we've been followed," he says quietly as we quickly enter the reception area.

I'm thinking that this place will cost us an arm and a leg. The interior is very attractive with rich dark wood paneling and recessed lighting as well as an ornate chandelier. We pass the entrance to a very posh restaurant as we enter. Fortunately, we are still dressed up in business attire or I think they would have tossed us out.

"What can we do for you?" asks a cute young Asian woman.

"We had to make an unscheduled stopover here in Seattle and would like a suite suitable for four adults. We'll need it for a week," I say very confidently. "We are going to be doing some business so we'll need more than one phone."

"I believe we have just what you want." She pulls a brochure from a rack and opens it to a very nice looking suite. "This suite comes with a multiline phone system and also has a great view of Puget Sound. Would you like to inspect the room first?" she asks.

I look at the picture holding it so Renee can see it too. "What do you think?" I ask Renee.

"If they provide a weekly discount, I think it will be just right," she answers.

"Of course we can do a discount. The regular price would be $175 a night but we can offer it for $125." She says confidently as she slides a registration slip across the desk. "How would you like to pay for that?"

I smile and break out four C notes and pass them back to her as take the registration form. "This will cover our first four days." I write in some totally bogus information and return the card.

"Thank you Mr. McCoy and Miss Chapel, I'm sure you will enjoy your stay. Our restaurant opens for dinner at 5:00; we have breakfast from 6:00 to 8:30 and lunch is available at 11:00 to 2:00." She hands us four keys. "Your room is on the 6th floor. The elevators are to your left and your room will be at the end of the hall to your right after you exit the elevator. Do your require help with your luggage?"

"No, Mr. Hernandez will bring it later." I take the keys and give one to Renee and one to Felipe and our little troupe heads for the elevator.

On the elevator Rene says, "McCoy, Chapel? What's our first names?"

"I'm Leonard and you're Christine, of course."

Renee hits me on the arm, "You didn't really do that, did you?"

"Ow! Yes I did, it was either that or Frank Burns and Hot Lips Houlihan," I reply as I rub my arm. "You want to be called Hot Lips?" I ask.

Renee pauses, then answers coyly, "Yeah, that might be fun."

I glance at Felipe and I catch him with his mouth wide open. It looks like he doesn't know if he should laugh or what.

We get to the room and it's all that the brochure said. I look out the window and it has a beautiful view of the Sound. It would be a whole lot nicer if it wasn't overcast and gray. It's amazing how fast the weather changes here.

"Felipe, can you stop by our apartment and bring some clothes? I don't think it's safe for us to show up there right now. You might want to stop and get some new luggage too. The suitcases we have would look pretty bad in this place." I hand Felipe the key to our apartment.

"Do you think you can get Rosie or someone to go with you?" asks Renee. "I'm not too keen on a guy picking out my wardrobe for the next week."

Felipe laughs, "Si, I wouldn't know what to pick up for you anyway. I'll try to get there before dark so we don't have to turn on a light and alert anyone who might be watching from the outside. I think you will be safe here but I better get going." Felipe keeps his hand out after taking the key.

"Oh, yeah," I pull out two hundreds and give them to him.

After Felipe leaves, Renee gets to work calling everyone in Rodney's books. I'm amazed at how easily it is for her to ask these guys to start sending checks to a post office box. Some ask a few questions but most must not think that someone could actually be stealing the checks. Maybe it's just me because of all the scams I've worked. Maybe they heard about the fire on Capitol Hill. Telling people the house burned down makes it easier.

I start working on the insurance for the house. First I call the fire chief to get some more information. He believes that the explosion was just a gas leak but they are still investigating. Next I dig through Rodney's papers and find his insurance agent and give him a call. He answers the phone and identifies himself with Tri State Insurance, an independent agent.

"Mr. Crothers, this is Darryl Smith. I'm working on behalf of your client, Rodney McNairy," I start off.

"Yes, Mr. Smith, what can I do for you?"

"Well, I've been going over some of Mr. McNairy's records that we were able to salvage from the fire and found that you are his insurance agent. Is that still correct?" I ask.

"Yes, Mr. McNairy has been a client of mine ever since his parents died about two years ago. But you mentioned a fire, what happened? Is he safe?" Crothers sounds alarmed on the phone.

"Yes, Mr. McNairy wasn't home at the time. We don't know exactly what happened but the fire department expects that there was a gas leak which exploded and essentially blew his house to smithereens. So, we need to get to work on seeing what his insurance will cover. When do you think you can get to work on that?" I ask.

There's a long pause on the other end of the line and Crothers starts talking, "Excuse me, this is quite a shock. I don't think I've had a client's house blow up before."

"Did I mention that it also caught on fire and that finished off anything that wasn't blown to bits?"

"Uh, well, I kind of assumed that. Anyway, I'll need to get some forms to Mr. McNairy for him to fill out, then I'll have to have an inspector look over the damage and assess it. This may take some time. How can I reach Mr. McNairy?" asks Crothers.

"That will be a bit of a problem as Mr. McNairy has had a medical problem and that's why I'm acting as his Power of Attorney at this time. I will be able to fill out any form you need and give you a copy of the Power of Attorney if you need it," I counter.

"Oh, I'm sorry; I didn't know anything was wrong with Mr McNairy. Of course I'll have the paper work delivered to you. Where can I send them?"

"Why don't you have the papers ready and I'll have someone come to your office and pick them up?" I don't want to give out our location to anyone.

"Certainly, Mr. Smith. It is getting a little late but I can have everything ready by 10:00 tomorrow morning. Will that work for you?" he asks.

"Yes, that will be fine. Thank you." I hang up.

I start working on the books along with Renee. After a couple of hours, we've contacted everyone and either have made the changes or arranged to pick up paperwork to finish it later.

I sit back in my chair and look at Renee after the last call. "So, not bad for a day's work, huh?"

"Whew, I don't know, Darryl. The way it went outside the stock broker's office, I never thought I'd end up in a fancy hotel room with such a devious man as you."

"You sweet talker you. Why don't we see just how nice these rooms are?" I ask as I get up and scoop her up in my arms.

"I thought you'd never ask."

I hear a knock at the door, let Renee go and look in the peephole. "It's Felipe the mood killer," I tell Renee and open the door.

"I heard that," says Felipe as he enters the room with two suitcases. "There are two more on the cart in the hall."

I step out and pick them up and bring them back in the room.

"That smaller one is your," he tells me as he points to one. "These others are all for Renee."

"That figures," I mumble. "Did you have any trouble?" I ask.

"No, I had someone stationed outside to make sure we were alone when we went into the apartment. I also had someone follow us to make sure we weren't tailed," explains Felipe. "You know, for a couple of con artists, you sure weren't living high on the hog," he changes the subject.

I wrinkle my nose and react, "Hey, we were doing all right. We got what we wanted."

"Well, now that you're in the big time, what are you going to do? You can't stay holed up in this place forever," Felipe states the obvious.

"Get yourself something to drink from the refrigerator and then sit down here with us and give us two amateurs some of your advice." I'm only half joking about being amateurs. Compared to what we normally do, we are going to need some big time advice. The Voice agrees.

Renee looks quizzically at me and I shrug my shoulders. I don't think she totally likes the idea of confiding in Felipe. I use a V gesture and point to my throat and she gets the idea.

We sit down in the plush chairs around a coffee table near the window. "So what is your assessment of the situation?" I ask.

"As I understand it, your amigo Rodney is going to be in danger as long as his will states Trickey is the executor of his estate. I also understand that you are going to be in danger as long as you have what Trickey feels is his money. The only think I can think of now is to somehow get Trickey to call off the dogs."

"Do you think if we set up a meeting we could buy him off?" asks Renee.

"Not likely. That would be a sign of weakness to go to him. If he's as crooked as we think, he won't honor any agreement and would just blackmail you for more," replies Felipe. "I keep thinking we need to eliminate Trickey."

"Whoa, man, I'm not going there. I'm not going to have anyone whacked. I will grab some loot and leave the rest to Trickey before I'll go for that," I adamantly state.

"Same here," agrees Renee.

"I'm not suggesting that even though it's what I think the guy deserves," says Felipe as he holds up his hand. "There has to be another way of getting him out of the picture."

The Voice gives me a suggestion.

"How did they get Al Capone?" I ask. "They never pinned anything on him for murder or any other crimes."

"Tax evasion," say Renee and Felipe together.

"Right. I'll bet that the records we got from Clarence would be enough to convince the IRS to look into Trickey's finances. If he was doing this to Rodney, he was probably doing it to others as well. All they need is a reason to subpoena his records." I feel good about this. Thanks, Voice.

"How do we get this information to the IRS without making ourselves vulnerable?" asks Renee.

"We could mail it to them anonymously," I suggest.

"We could plant it where they might find it themselves," says Felipe.

"What do you mean?" I ask.

"Well, suppose someone knew of an FBI raid that was about to happen and the reports were confiscated?" says Felipe with a cunning smile.

"OK, so how long would it take them to discover the reports among all the other evidence they take? It would have to stand out and be evident that this was worth following up," I say with some skepticism. I know how slow the government moves. I'm not real thrilled about hiding out for months.

"Would there be some way of implicating Trickey along with whatever reason they might be doing the original raid?" asks Renee. "These reports don't have his name on them so it would take a while for the feds to get the connection."

"That's a good idea," I say. "Dang, I should have had you pick up Renee's typewriter and the files we use. We'll need those to establish the connection. Oh, we'll also need a new Slecetric ball that we can toss afterwards. We don't want them tracing anything back to us."

"Sure, I can pick up those things tomorrow," agrees Felipe.

"What kind of raid were you thinking about?" I ask. "We know that Rodney's broker was up to his neck in gambling debts. That's how Trickey hooked him into cheating. Would a gambling raid do it?"

"Hmm, that might work, but if they thought they could get some evidence of money laundering along with the raid, it would boost it higher on their priority list," says Felipe thoughtfully.

"Yeah, that would work. If they are looking for evidence of money laundering and find information connecting Trickey to the accounts on the transfers they'll want to dig deeper." I'm liking this more and more as we go.

"How do we know where a raid is going to go down and how do we plant the documents?" asks Renee.

"Details, details, Renee. Why do you need to know details?" asks Felipe but he continues before Renee can react and knock his block off. I'm the only one she would let get away with that. "The raid will be the result of an anonymous tip. That's the easy part. The hard part will be planting the evidence without getting caught."

"I'm not in the gambling circuit, so where do we plant the documents?" I ask.

"There are a number of gambling organizations in Seattle so I'll have to find out who is linked to Trickey. Then I'll have to get someone I can trust who isn't known by that mob to do some gambling. They don't exactly like to see the competition in their establishments," explains Felipe. "Once inside, they case the joint to see where to plant the documents. Hopefully, they can spot an office."

Felipe pauses for a long time.

"OK, how do they get the stuff into the office? If there is gambling going on, isn't there going to be guards and a lot of people around?" asks Renee.

"I'm thinking, I'm thinking," replies Felipe, a bit annoyed.

I'm thinking too. I'm thinking Felipe is stuck and doesn't know how to pull it off.

"Why don't we just mail it to them?" asks Renee. "We put it in an envelope marked, 'to be opened only by Trickey.' Put that inside another envelope and mail it to the address of the joint."

"That would be too easy. Besides, why would they not open it or even forward it to Trickey?" asks Felipe.

I interrupt, "Renee and I will take it in. She's the decoy because she's downright knock-down gorgeous when she wants to distract dumb goons. And I have some ways of persuasion to get into the office and stash the documents in a place the feds will find it but won't require any of the mob guys to know it's there. We'll still need your guy to case the joint." The Voice's plan, not mine.

Renee starts to protest but I just give her the V sign. Felipe is speechless.

"Fine, I can go with that," says Renee calmly.

"Are you loco? These guys are looking for you and you're going to walk into their joint?" Felipe is a bit disturbed by the idea, as I would expect.

"Oh, you really care for us, don't you, Felipe?" I ask.

"Ha, not all that much, but think of how much I'd lose if they whack you," says Felipe with a bit of disgust.

"Not to worry, your financial stake will be secure. We've done enough masquerades that they won't recognize us. And I think you know that I can be very persuasive, don't you?" I ask as I give him just a glimpse of The Voice's power. "Maybe it's time for you to get cracking on finding the ideal place for the raid."

Felipe seems a bit befuddled but gets up and excuses himself, "Yeah, I think I need to find an ideal place for the raid." He heads out the door without another word.

"Wow! That was pretty impressive, Darryl. I assume you attribute that to The Voice?" asks Renee.

"Yeah, and that was on the low power setting too."

"Well, more power to The Voice," she says enthusiastically.

Chapter Eleven

It's been a long boring day sitting in the hotel room. Some of Felipe's guys have been dropping by with forms to fill out that they picked up from some of Rodney's accounts. The one from the insurance agent didn't look all that bad but it was still boring. Renee and I are both starting to feel like we need to get out for a while, but we've even been ordering room service to keep from being spotted.

Felipe stopped by once and was pretty antsy. Apparently the scuttlebutt on the street is that Trickey's guys are still actively looking for us. So there is always one of Felipe's guys in our room, even last night. That made things a bit awkward even though the suite is set up for two couples.

The afternoon drags on into evening and we decide to turn in.

Funny how being bored can make me tired. Before I drift off, I think about how freaked out some of my high school friends would be if they knew I was listening to a voice, much less doing what it said. This would all seem too much like Rosemary's Baby to them. They would be sure I was involved in some kind of Satanic cult. I drop off to sleep real fast.

I wake up in the middle of the night and hear some hushed voices in the other room. I quietly get out of bed and slowly open the door. In the next room I see Felipe, Rosie, and the back of another person I don't recognize. They are on their knees around the coffee table with a single small candle burning on the table. It clearly illuminates their faces even though they have dark hoods over their heads. Their voices are all blended together into what sounds like a singsong Latin chant that I remember hearing during Mass as a kid.

Rosie reaches for a chalice on one side of the table and places it in front of her. She then produces a small rodent from somewhere I couldn't see. She quickly slits its throat and drains the blood into the chalice. I want to scream but I'm frozen, like in a dream. She then pours some of the blood into the chalices that the other two hold up. I can see the third person's hand extending from the sleeve of his robe, boney with claw-like fingernails. They each drink the blood down.

Felipe turns and looks at me with an evil smile as the third person stands and turns toward me. His face is hidden away from the candle but I can see his eyes glowing. I'm no longer frozen as I scream and run back into our room, quickly locking the door.

Renee jumps out of bed yelling, asking what's going on. I just grab her by the hand and yell we need to get out of here. We burst through the door into the hallway and turn toward the elevators only to be met by two of Trickey's goons with drawn pistols. They start running toward us and we duck back around the corner to the stairs. We pull the door open and slam it behind us. I grab a mop that is leaning against the wall and jam it through the door handle.

We start down the stairwell as fast as we can but stop suddenly as we see the haunting figure who was in the other room coming up the stairs toward us. We turn and run up the stairs past the door to our floor and toward the roof. The mop handle is starting to break as we go up the stairs and the footsteps of the creature are getting closer. The lights in the stairwell go out as the banging on the door gets louder and louder. I'm grabbed from behind and shaken.

Renee whispers in my ear as she gently shakes me, "Wake up Darryl, what's going on out there?"

OK, I'm really awake now and the thumping is coming from the hallway. We get up and open the door to the main room of the suite. Our night guy is standing beside the door with his automatic drawn. He motions us to get back in our room but just then the door flies open with two wrestling bodies following and crashing to the floor. Our guy kicks the door closed and whacks one of the two on the head with his gun. Fight over.

I'm standing there in my briefs, jaw dropped.

Our outside guy gets up rubbing his jaw and kicks the down guy in the head while muttering curses, I presume, in Spanish. But the guy on the floor isn't out! He pulls a gun and quickly shoots our guys. Blood splatters all over the ceiling as the bullets rip upward though their skulls.

Not a dream! But I react just as I did in the dream; I turn and pull Renee back into our room, bolting the door behind us. We open the door to the hall only to have the creature laughing in our faces.

We run to the window. I hope there is a fire escape outside. No such luck. We both turn as the door to the other room opens and the downed guy with the gun steps in. But it isn't the guy with the gun, instead it is a bearded person with a white robe. He holds one hand up to the creature at the door and states firmly, "They aren't yours yet. Get out of here." The creature disappears in a puff of smoke.

I sit up straight in bed with a start. My heart is racing. Renee is also sitting upright.

"What's going on?" she asks.

"I don't know about you but I think I just had a double nightmare," I answer.

"No, what's going on out there? Didn't you hear the commotion in the hall? It sounded like gunshots but not that loud," she whispers.

I hear quiet talking in the other room so we get up and peek into the other room. Our night guy is talking with someone at the door. The door closes, then he starts to walk toward our room. We back off and away from the bed. He knocks on the door.

"Senor, Senorita," he calls.

"What's going on," I answer.

"I'm afraid that your enemies have found you. We have silenced the threat, but we need to move quickly before more come back," he answers.

"So the noise in the hall?" asks Renee.

"Si, there was an intruder who unfortunately was shot but escaped."

"OK, we're getting dressed and we'll pack up everything and be ready to go in five minutes."

I look at the clock and it's 2:11 in the morning. What a miserable time to be doing a crash packing. We scramble around, stuffing our bags from the dresser drawers. The paperwork all fits in Renee's briefcase. I wished we had a case to put the Selectric in. That is one heavy typewriter. It takes us eleven and a half minutes to pack and we get done just before we hear a knock on the door.

Our night guy looks through the peephole and then opens the door. Two guys come in. They are dressed in white shirts, black pants, and tattered denim jackets. One of them hands Renee and me an outfit that looks a lot like theirs. "Try these on," he says. They each load up with suitcases and leave.

We go back into the bedroom and put them on. Renee has a black skirt instead of pants. I have a scruffy looking plaid jacket, but she has a nice looking black coat. We both have baseball caps that can partially hide our faces. After we're changed, we bring our regular clothes out and pack them in the last suitcase. The typewriter and briefcase are both gone. I'm a bit concerned about losing track of the briefcase.

Our night guys says, "As soon as Armando gets back, he and the others – there will be another senorita with you – they will escort you out the back into the alley. With these clothes and the others who will meet you there, it will look just like you just got off work at a restaurant or the hotel."

Four of us go down the service elevator to the basement, exit, and make our way through the laundry to the rear alley exit. When we step into the alley, we are surrounded by three other guys and two women. We all walk about a block to a bus stop. The other guys and gals are loudly talking in Spanish as we walk. We have to wait for about fifteen minutes until a bus arrives. We all pile on and congregate in the back. There is only one other person on the bus, a smelly older man who reeks of alcohol. He avoids eye contact.

The bus takes us to Denny Way heading west, to First Ave North then a slight jog on Roy before we head up the hill on Queen Anne Ave. We exit the bus across the street from a 7-Eleven. When the bus pulls away, we jay-walk across the street, then make our way between the 7-Eleven and the apartment building beside it. In the alley behind the apartment building, a car is waiting for us. One of the guys opens the back door.

I say, "Thank for the escort."

He replies, "Por nada."

Renee gets in first and slides across to the passenger side, and then I get in.

"It took you guys long enough to get here," says the driver.

"Yeah, Felipe, do you know how cold those buses are this time of the morning? Pretty clever exit plan. Thanks, man," I reply, relieved to see a familiar face.

"I'm concerned about our luggage. Do you know where it is?" asks Renee.

"Si, it is about to arrive at the airport aboard a Sorrento courtesy van, with a suspicious black car following it," replies Felipe. "However, your briefcase with all your paperwork is here in the passenger seat." He pulls out of the alley and turns left on West Garfield.

"Oh, whew," I let out a long breath of air. "Where are we headed now?" I ask.

"We have a place we believe will be safe. It isn't as nice as the Sorrento, but we can make sure you are safe there."

We go a few blocks west, north and then start down the hill on Gilman Drive. Part way down, we make a left on 12th and stop in front of a shack on our right that looks like it is ready to slip off the hill. The hill is so steep here that the street is split in two with one lane about ten feet higher than the other side above us on the left.

Felipe points to a black van parked on the upper side of the street, "Those are our amigos. There will always be someone there with a vantage point on the street. The only bad part of this is that it is a dead end, but they have a perfect view of the street from there."

We get out of the car and Felipe leads us, not to the main entrance, which is level with the street, but down steps beside the house to a hidden lower level. "Our guys will also be in the upper level of the house if you need them. Just use a broom stick to pound on the ceiling."

We enter the lower apartment but I can see the steps going down further. "What's below us?"

"There is storage at the very back below here. Between you and the next street down there is a very steep twenty-foot incline covered in blackberries. There are trees at the edge of the next street so you can't even see the house from there," explains Felipe as he turns on a light as we step into the kitchen.

"How did they know where we were?" I ask.

"We think they must have followed one of the couriers who picked up paperwork and delivered it to you yesterday. I have a hunch it was the insurance agent," replies Felipe.

"If he did it, we need to find out for sure before we give him any more opportunities to find us. We'll have some forms and things ready to take back to all of Rodney's accounts tomorrow. We'll include the post office address for mailing but provide a note with a fake address for our location. You can have someone watch to see if anyone shows up."

"Good idea, Felipe. Do you know of a cheap motel along 99? We have six accounts that wanted paperwork and Crothers makes seven. So it has to be a place with at least 7 rooms visible from the street. We give each account a different room number and see if any goons show up there," offers Rene.

"Si, there is a transient motel north of Seattle that I know about. I'll call you in the morning with the address," says Felipe.

"Great, speaking of morning, I'm beat but I'm not sure I can get any sleep. Is that the bedroom to the right?"

"Si, and I'm sorry about your clothes, but we may not be able to retrieve them. They will be watching them," says Felipe.

"Well, I guess it's time for a new wardrobe, but if we are holing up here, how will we get any time to shop?" asks Renee.

"I'll have Rosie stop by with some catalogs. She can take your measurements and get what you want," says Felipe.

"Make sure she gets one with some fancy evening wear. I'll need something special for our undercover work," says Renee with a gleam in her eye.

I can see her now in that gambling joint with every eye on her. Yeah, she'll do fine.

Chapter Twelve

It's almost 5:00 AM before we are able to get into bed. This shack is incredible. The back bedroom appears to have been built by enclosing a porch. There are lots of windows and it is cold in here. The floor slants downward toward the back of the house by at least six inches just in the length of the bed. Fortunately, we have our head on the upward side of the room.

Renee falls asleep quickly but I'm running over the night in my mind. The dreams before I finally woke up are haunting. Was this a warning like when I was meditating or do dreams even mean anything?

I remember the stories I heard in church about people interpreting dreams. They all meant something. What was one of those, three and twenty black birds baked in a pie? No, that was a nursery rhyme. Oh, yeah, it was a dream a baker had about birds eating the bread that was on top of his head or something like that. It meant he was going to be beheaded.

If my dreams meant anything, what would it be? Well, my dream about the stockbroker turned out to be way too real.

I'm startled awake by loud knocking at the door. I look at my watch and see that it's 10:12 AM. Where am I? Nothing looks familiar. I close my eyes and the knocking starts again. Renee screams, "Stop it already! Give us a minute and we'll be there."

OK, I'm awake and know where we are. We're in the shack on the side of Queen Anne Hill that will slide off if we jump up and down on the floor. Or maybe just the bedroom will break off.

I get out of bed, pull on my pants, and put on the white shirt and jacket. It's really cold in this bedroom. I go out and turn left to go though the kitchen, then open the door for Felipe.

"Come on in," I moan. That bed left more kinks in me than I ever imagined I could have. I thought the Murphy bed in our apartment was bad.

"Did you sleep well?" asks Felipe.

I just look at him for a few seconds, "Have you ever slept here?" I ask.

"No."

"Then you should try it sometime and then you wouldn't bother asking."

"Oh, that bad. Let me get some coffee started. That might cheer you up," he offers.

"That would be good."

Renee comes out of the bedroom. Wow, she looks like a mess, not that I'd ever tell her. She scowls at Felipe and brushes past us into the bathroom.

"Renee's going to want to get some new clothes soon. How's that going?" I ask. I don't want to have to deal with her when she's in a bad mood. "You better have some good news."

"Si, Rosie will be here very shortly and will be able to get a few things quickly," replies Felipe.

"Well, that's some good news."

"I have some bad news though," says Felipe with a smile as Renee comes out of the bathroom.

"You what?" she asks. "Since when do people smile when they have bad news?"

Felipe flops a newspaper on the table and points to a picture of a smashed up van. "It appears that you both died last night."

I think my eyes pop out as I see the word "Sorrento" on the side of the van. "Holy cow, what happened?"

"The article says that a semi forced the van off the road. Witnesses say it was a hit and run. The driver was ok but the two passengers were tossed around so much that they didn't survive. They were identified by their luggage. It says they are you two," recounts Felipe.

"Were they your people?" I ask. No; why would he smile if they were?

"I don't know who they were. We had two of ours get in the van at the hotel but blocked it from view with a garbage truck just after it passed the alley, where they got out and rode the garbage truck. There shouldn't have been anyone in the van except the driver. We're sure it worked because the suspicious black car continued to follow it." Felipe shrugs his shoulders as he explains.

It is just too early for me to make sense of this.

"Maybe they were your guardian angels." This time he makes a sign of the cross with his right hand.

Yeah, just like some of the superstitious Catholics I grew up with. They believe in angels, go to confession, and shoot someone the next day. "Give me a break. You don't really believe that, do you?" I respond.

"No, think about it, Darryl. What happened to the two people who got into our car before it blew up? Now two more people are killed who appear to be us," says Renee.

Felipe crosses himself again and loses a bit of color in his face. "Madre mia! This has happened before?"

I roll my eyes and answer, "Yeah, our car didn't just blow up, two people who looked like us got into it just before it went up in smoke. But, I'm pretty sure that the answer doesn't lie with angels. There must be some logical explanation for both of these situations. Maybe we didn't really see what we thought. The couple in the van may have been someone that was a last minute addition by the hotel. I wouldn't get all excited about it." I give the V sign to Renee.

"Yeah, you're probably right," agrees Renee. "That couple could have gotten in the car just in front of ours or maybe continued up the street." She shakes her head. "It's really terrible, though, that the couple got caught in the van."

"Si, maybe you are right," says Felipe. I don't think he's totally convinced.

Rosie arrives and takes Renee into the living room to look over the catalogs she brought while Felipe and I stay in the kitchen and have a cup of coffee.

"My people have been hitting the streets and finding out all we can about Trickey and his organization. It appears that we may have underestimated the mob he's associated with," says Felipe.

"What do you mean? How have you underestimated them?" I ask. These are not words I like to hear when running a scam, much less when someone is out to kill me.

"You see, before this broke loose, we didn't even know about Trickey. It seems that he is not simply associated with this mob, but he runs it and also has significant interest in the local Chinese mob. We aren't sure how, but it's possible he also runs it. Until now he has been successful keeping out of sight. Since you can connect him to ripping off Rodney, it isn't just about money anymore; you are a serious threat."

Now it's my turn to be alarmed. "So you're saying that Trickey is way more powerful than you expected?"

"Si, that is true," replies Felipe.

"Do you have any really good news this morning? I mean other than we are dead so they may not be looking for us?" I ask. "Oh by the way, that isn't really great news as that means if Trickey can verify our deaths, then our Power of Attorney is useless."

"Oh, I hadn't thought of that," admits Felipe. "Well, maybe the good news is that with his Chinese connection, we can infiltrate a gambling den in the International District. You would be less likely to be recognized there."

"Yeah, that might work, as long as they have white customers. If we walk in and everyone else is Chinese, we might not even get in the door.

"When I was in the Navy, our ship stopped in Hong Kong for leave. I went with some buddies to Kowloon. It was late and we were getting hungry so we went in a door of a restaurant. The door opened directly to stairs and down to a lower room. We got down far enough to see across the smoke filled room. Every eye in the place was on us and not one was blue. I've never felt more unwelcome as that. We immediately backed up the stairs and returned to Hong Kong."

"Si, I know what you mean. I feel the same quite often even here in Seattle, but it is the gringo restaurants where I feel that way," says Felipe.

"Touché. We are still a long ways from what we should be," I acknowledge. "We are going to need to act soon, though, or it may be too late."

I'm interrupted by the phone ringing. "Well, it can't be for me," I say. "Nobody's supposed to know I'm here, I haven't been on the phone, and I'm dead."

"Si, it is probably for me." Felipe answers the phone and starts speaking in Spanish.

With three years of Spanish in school, I still can't keep up with the spoken language. I may as well have never taken the classes. Felipe hangs up the phone.

"Do you want the good news or the bad news?" he asks.

I just shake my head back and forth, "Just out with it."

"Good news is that you aren't dead. In fact, no one is dead. My friends who work in the morgue assured me that no one was brought in from any accidents last night. Not in Seattle, or anywhere near the airport. They said a wagon showed up at the right time and was supposed to have two bodies but when they opened the door, there were only two empty body bags. There was no sign of tampering. After questioning the driver he swears that they were there when he left the accident scene. He didn't make any stops except for traffic lights."

"Holy cow! Maybe your guardian angel theory is correct," says Renee who just stepped back into the kitchen along with Rosie when Felipe hung up. She says it with a wink at me.

Rosie crosses herself.

Felipe crosses himself. "It is verdad; you have someone looking out for you that can do more than we can. I also inquired if he heard of any other things like this happening and he said the same thing happened two days ago. The burnt bodies of two people from a car fire also disappeared in route to the morgue. There wasn't even any sign inside the body bags that anything had been in them."

"So that's good news also because Trickey can't prove we're dead," says Renee.

"And the bad news is that he will still be out there looking for us," I respond.

Felipe just says, "Si!" It looks like he has a lot on his mind.

"On a lighter note, how are you and Rosie doing on the wardrobe?" I ask.

"We have picked out a lovely wardrobe for Renee," answers Rosie. "However, it will be rather expensive," she adds.

"Oh, well, I hope it isn't too much. Our cash reserves are getting rather low. If Trickey has any smarts, he probably knows where Rodney's accounts are sending their payments, most of which won't be due for a while anyway, so he's watching for anyone to pick them up. I don't want to show up at the bank in person and they probably won't cash one of the temporary checks we got when we opened the account. At least not for any significant amount. How much do we have left?" I ask Renee.

She leaves the room and comes back with a thick envelope that had the C notes from the safe. "We've used about $4,000 in the past two days just for cars and payment for Felipe's guys," she says. "That leaves about $10,000."

"That's not going to last long at this rate," I grumble. "Rosie, do you still have the diamonds? They never did make it back to us."

"Si, we still have them," she answers.

"Good, we may need to sell some until we can come out of hiding. In the mean time, Renee, take what you need for the clothes. Our number one priority is to take Trickey down as soon as possible." Gads, I sound almost like I know what I'm doing.

I watch Renee calmly peel off ten C notes from the stack and hand them to Rosie. I hold my tongue, which isn't what I'm used to. Then I remember, "Hey Rosie, don't forget I need some new clothes before these rot on me."

Rosie winks and holds up one C note, "Si, this is for you. But we do need to get you measured." She whips out a tape measure from her purse along with a notebook. She hands the tape to Renee and I'm thankful for that, not that Rosie isn't a good-looking lady and she is older. I just don't want to have to deal with Renee afterwards.

"I will be back this afternoon with your new clothes," says Rosie as she leaves by the kitchen door.

"I need to get going also," says Felipe. "I need to make sure we have the best gambling location scouted out." He starts to leave.

"Just a minute," I stop him, "I think we need to get those diamonds back in our possession." I give him a stern look just to make sure I'm not kidding.

"Hmm, I think we still need to keep them as a retainer, just in case you can't pay up later," replies Felipe.

The Voice tells me to let him keep half, but not make it easy.

"I can deal with a retainer, say, thirty percent?" I offer.

"How about sixty percent?" replies Felipe.

"Fifty?" I respond.

"Agreed. I'll bring half of them with me this afternoon."

I smile, it could have been harder, but I know that The Voice could have made sure he complied. "We'll see you this afternoon, then."

Felipe leaves and Renee asks, "Fifty percent of the diamonds? That's got to be about $125,000."

I shrug, "Yeah, it seems like a lot but that's what The Voice said. Besides, they are doing a lot and if something should happen to us, they'd lose their investment, so to speak."

"I don't want to hear anything about something happening to us," says Renee with a shudder.

"I hear you, but our foray into enemy territory will be risky," I comment casually.

"Stop it!" says Renee as she stomps her foot. "Don't talk that way."

"OK, OK," I throw up my hands. "Jeeze, don't blow a gasket."

"Well, I need to get cleaned up. There are a couple of bathrobes in there," she points to the bathroom. "I want to get out of these clothes." She starts for the bathroom.

"We could do that together," I say.

"Yeah, let's," she responds with a smile.

Chapter Thirteen

At 4:30 Felipe and Rosie come back with our new duds – and the diamonds. I'm just thankful to get some clean clothes on. Renee has been running around the house with just the bathrobe on but I didn't feel comfortable and kept on the clothes from last night.

While Rosie and Renee are trying on the tons of clothes Rosie brought back for her, Felipe and I go over the plans to plant the stock reports in one of Trickey's gambling parlors.

"Here's what we found. Trickey has several rooms in the International District, but his high stakes room is between 510 and 512 7th Ave. It's an old brick building that is quite large. There is an emergency exit on 7th which appears to be the front of the building. The real entrance is on Canton Alley at the back of the building. There are several small shops there and each is a front. You have to know which one to enter any specific day and you need to know a password, which also changes each day," explains Felipe.

"So you were able to penetrate and get all this information to get in?" I ask.

"Si, but it wasn't easy and it wasn't cheap," says Felipe. "Our guy managed to get in but he wasn't able to stay long. After he got in, a bouncer as big as a Sumo wrestler said he didn't recognize him. He started asking questions about how he found out about the joint. Our guy was quite good, but when the bouncer asked to see his stake, our guy couldn't produce enough and was escorted out."

"How about the other customers? Was it a mix of people or were they all Oriental?" I ask.

"There were primarily Orientals but there were a few white people. No Mexicans which is probably why my guy was quickly singled out," answered Felipe. "However, he did manage to scout out the place and drew up a floor plan of the main room. We also got the building plans from the city and pieced together as much as we could. Some of the pieces don't fit so I think there must have been some changes that aren't on the city blueprints."

"Yeah, that makes sense, especially if they have something to hide," I can see from the drawings that there are several possible locations for their main office. "Is there a basement? What's the possibility that one of these doors leads downstairs and that's where the office is?" I want to make sure I don't have to go to a place where I can get trapped easily.

Felipe laughs, "You don't know much about Seattle history do you? Seattle is famous for its underground tours. Even this far back from the waterfront, there are long lost passages and rooms under most of the buildings. The Chinese were not always welcome. The tunnels and rooms under the area were used for opium dens, gambling, and even torture. We made sure that we picked a place that wasn't underground, but the office could be."

"Oh swell, I take the wrong door and end up on a rack," I comment even though I'm not worried about it.

"Probably not. Our guy did have enough time to see the employee traffic. His guess is that this door leads to the office. He wasn't able to determine if it went downstairs or not."

"It looks like there is at least twenty feet from this door to the end of the building that faces 7th Ave. Is that right?" I ask.

"Si, it could be more or less because the measurements were taken from the city's plans. There is plenty of room for the office to be there," answers Felipe.

"I think we'll be able to take care of this," I say confidently. "You will be able to get the correct entrance and the password for tomorrow night, won't you?"

"Si, they change in the afternoon, but we should be able to get the information before you arrive. When do you plan to go in?" asks Felipe.

"That depends on the timing of the raid. I want to be in there about thirty minutes before and be out at least ten minutes before," I reply.

"Whew, that might be hard to do. We can't even guarantee that the cops will act on our tip, much less time the raid," says Felipe.

"You have primed them, haven't you?" I ask, just a bit irritated. "I thought this part was better organized."

"Si, we have let them know that they will have an opportunity to make a major bust, but they have to be secretive also, otherwise the gambling parlor will find out and just be a restaurant when they show up," explains Felipe.

I look up from the dining room table as Renee catches my eye. She is modeling her red evening dress. It is tight in all the right places and loose where it will attract much attention; short, too. I knew she could really look great dressed up, but this outfit, no, the way she's wearing it makes me speechless. "Wow," I finally utter.

Felipe turns around and after he catches his breath, whistles. "I can see why she would distract them."

"You can stop drooling now," she says as she goes back in the bedroom.

"And just exactly how is she going to hide a ream of papers in that dress?" asks Felipe.

"I hope Rose bought a huge matching handbag," I say while still staring at the closed door. "On second thought, maybe I can take a briefcase with money on top. With Renee leading the way, they won't pay much attention and only see the bills on top. The rest can be ones underneath."

"I think I have just the briefcase you need," says Felipe. "It has a false bottom that isn't too obvious but should hold the stock reports without being seen."

"Excellent! With the exception of timing, I think we're ready to go."

Felipe and Rosie leave about 6:00 PM and we have the evening to ourselves. It seems like it has been forever since we had a quiet evening.

It feels good to have a lot more room than our apartment on the Ave. We have a couch, a couple of overstuffed chairs, and a decent TV here with color. It's all second hand stuff but still a lot better than home.

After dinner, I turn on the TV and plop down on the couch. Renee joins me as the set warms up and the picture comes on well after the sound. It's a Star Trek re-run. The one where they try to go through the barrier at the edge of the galaxy and something happens to one of Kirk's friends and shipmate, Gary Mitchell. The guy gets all these super powers but it all goes to his head and he thinks he is a god. It took us no more than thirty seconds of the opening scene to remember it.

"Let's watch something else. We've seen this at least three times," says Renee.

"Yeah, but this is in color," I protest. I feel strangely drawn to the character of Gary and want to watch it again. I wonder just how far the relationship with The Voice would be able to take me, especially after seeing the way I can give people a look and they suddenly comply with my requests.

My protest goes unheeded as Renee gets up and changes the channel.

"What's this?" I ask. "Is that a religious show?"

"It looks like a Billy Graham crusade to me," says Renee. "I've always wondered what they were all about. Let's watch."

"Is he something like Oral Roberts?" I ask. I remember when I was a kid; our family went to visit my grandmother and aunt. They had their TV running and this guy was preaching in a tent. People came up to him at the end and he would put his hands on their heads and pray for them. It was really weird; I never heard anyone make such noisy prayers. It was also weird because my grandmother was a staunch Catholic. At that age, I remember being told that I shouldn't even walk on the same side of the street as a protestant church or the devil might come out and get me. I guess he was OK if she watched him.

The Voice tells me that this isn't something I should watch.

Oddly enough, I ask why. I don't think I've ever questioned him before.

The Voice tells me that it is nothing but lies and philosophies intended to keep people from developing their true potential. It is a form of oppression that has kept mankind from doing far more than anyone ever thought possible.

"Jesus is the only way to the Father," comes from the TV.

You hear that lie? Not only is it a lie but who cares about the Christian's father? If mankind only knew that they could all become gods.

You mean like Gary Mitchell in the Star Trek show? I ask.

That, of course, is just what the writers could imagine about how a human being would be corrupted by such powers, The Voice continues. *In their imagination they can't come close to what you could become.*

Wow, that's quite impressive, but I've never seen or read of anyone with powers like this, I respond.

That's because Christianity has suppressed any mention of it and has even killed people with these powers out of fear. They take shows like Star Trek and twist it to make it seem like mankind can't handle the power, that it is evil and then they kill those headed in that path, just like Kirk killed Gary Mitchell, who once was his friend.

Yeah, I guess that makes sense, I ponder.

"Jesus Christ died for your sins. He took your punishment on Himself," comes from the TV.

So what about sins? I ask The Voice.

Sins are in your mind and imagination, it responds. *While there are certainly things that are wrong, any eternal punishment for them is just another scare tactic used to make you conform to the rules of the church,* The Voice explains.

That sounds right with what I experienced. What about eternal punishment and hell? I was always told that if I had a mortal sin on my soul when I died, I would go to hell. The guy on TV said Jesus' death paid for the penalty of my sins. OK, they aren't sins but if I were a murderer and suddenly died, what happens?

There is no hell, says The Voice. *When you die, if you have been following a path to enlightenment, as I had, then you shed your physical body and become a spirit like me. The bad things are behind you and now you have the ability to help others in various ways, as I've been helping you.*

Whoa, you were once a man? I ask The Voice.

Renee hits me on the arm, "Hey did you fall asleep?"

"No, I was just thinking," I answer.

"Well you could have fooled me. What did you think about Billy Graham?" she asks.

The program is over? Wow time went fast. "I think all that religion stuff is made up to just keep the powerful people on top or as a crutch for weak people," I answer.

"Hmm, you may be right," she says but I can tell that it wasn't a very enthusiastic agreement. "What if he's right, if there is a God and our relationship with Jesus makes the difference between eternity in heaven or hell?"

"There is no hell; it's just made up to scare you into conformity," I answer with confidence.

"How can you be so confident of that?" Renee asks.

I roll my eyes but regret that I did it as her set jaw tells me it was a mistake. "The Voice has assured me of that," I answer.

"OK," she nods her head slowly. That's not a good sign. "And how does he know this?"

"Because he was once a man, died and is now a spirit," I answer even though it doesn't sound as convincing as when he said it.

"What if he's one of those evil spirits that rebelled against God and is now just trying to mess with us?" asks Renee.

"Where did you get that?" I ask, getting a little irritated here.

"From the TV. Now I'm sure you were asleep," she accuses me.

"I did too hear the TV. I heard that Jesus thinks He's the only way to God and that Billy Graham thinks that we'll go to hell if we don't believe in Jesus. It's all just a bunch of crap." I get up and storm out through the kitchen and into the bathroom. I don't want to hear any more of this nonsense.

I told you not to watch that show, says The Voice.

"Oh, shut up!" I say aloud, thankful that Renee wasn't in earshot.

When I return, which isn't quickly, Renee is watching another show. When I come in, she doesn't say a word but has a smirk on her face. She won the button pushing war.

Chapter Fourteen

It's a warm evening for April, which is good, otherwise I think Renee would freeze in her bare shoulder dress, even though she has a wrap. We are only a couple of minutes from the International District and our plan to drop the evidence against Tickey in the office of the gambling room.

"Have I told you how great you look tonight?" I ask.

"Just about a million times, Lover Boy," she answers. "Now just make sure I don't distract you when we get there."

"Yeah, that might be a problem," I say as I lean over closer to her in the back seat of the limo.

"Hey, we don't need any drool on the dress," she teases.

We arrive in the alley and the limo stops by one of the doors. The driver says, "This is the door for tonight. The password is Kowloon."

"Thanks, as soon as we walk through the door, we're on the clock. We should come out the back in precisely twenty minutes," I answer and open the limo's door. I get out and hold the door as Renee slips out. I open the door to the little shop and nod to the driver. He moves on as we enter.

The place certainly doesn't look like the entrance to anything. It is cluttered with paper lanterns hanging from the ceiling. There are ceramic dragons, and all sorts of other touristy things in the shop. In a way, it kind of reminds me of Joe's apothecary. An old Chinese man comes out from behind a display case.

"How can I help you?" he asks.

"Do you know how to get to Kowloon?" I answer.

There is just a hint of surprise on his face, but he isn't looking at me. "Follow me," he says.

We go behind the display case and he reaches around the corner. I hear a click and the wall rotates inward away from us, shelves and all. It's the only way it could go with the clutter in the shop. Smart too; it doesn't leave a scratch on the floor. He gestures for us to go in.

We walk through the door into a small room with a very unfriendly looking bouncer. He's big too; his black suit coat doesn't fit around his stomach. I wonder if this is the guy that kicked Felipe's scout out. There's a curtained door at the end of the room and a small table by one wall. The lighting is low but the Chinese motif is clearly evident. The sounds of a casino are coming from the behind the curtain.

The bouncer points to the table but his eyes are on Renee. I put my briefcase on it and step back. He opens it, glances at the stack of money, and then closes it. With a smile he beckons us toward the curtain. He draws it back and follows us into the gambling parlor.

A short Chinese man in a very well tailored black suit approaches us. It looks like black suits are the uniform for the joint's employees. "Welcome to our club. May I be of assistance?" he asks.

"If you don't mind, I'd like to look around a bit and see where we might best enjoy your facility," I answer. I don't want to rush in but most importantly to make sure Renee is seen. "Then I'll need some chips."

The short guy looks at the bouncer who nods slightly.

"Of course, please feel free to take your time," he answers and steps back.

Renee and I make a circuit of the club, stopping at different tables to see what the layout is like. They have it all, except for slot machines. We stop at a black jack table near the cashier's window and the door to the office.

"I think I would like to try this, Sugar," she says.

"A good choice, my dear. You can start with this while I get some chips," I'm trying to talk sophisticated but not sure it's coming off. It doesn't matter; most people are looking at Renee. I hand her five hundred and then walk to the cashier's window. There is some appreciative murmuring from the table as Renee takes a seat.

She takes off her wrap and every goon in the place is watching her. Exactly what I wanted. I try the door to the office but it is locked. So I continue to the window.

"May I help you?" asks the woman behind the bars.

"Yes, I have a hefty amount of cash here that needs to be converted. I would like to make sure you can handle this discreetly and in private, in the office," I state emphatically.

"I'm sorry sir, but that won't be possible. Only employees are allowed in the office," she answers politely.

I smile, then give her the look. "I think now would be a good time to buzz me in."

She frowns with a puzzled look but presses the buzzer to unlock the door. "Of course, sir, go on in."

I look around and no one is watching me, as planned. However, another big guy greets me inside the door and before I know it, I'm staring down the barrel of a 45. "Who are you and how did you get in here?" he demands.

"I'm here to personally ensure this cash with your boss," I reply as calmly as I can. I lift the briefcase slightly.

"Do that at the window. No one comes in here, and I mean no one." He flips the barrel of the gun toward the door.

OK Voice, this had better work. It's what you told me would work. I take a deep breath and give him as cold a look as I can muster, squinting, and clenching my teeth as I speak. "No, you will lower your gun and let me pass. I also want you to make sure that your boss doesn't pull a gun out of his desk."

His eyes glass over but he quickly turns and aims his gun toward the back of the room. "Hands out where I can seem them, Chang," he yells, then steps aside.

I can now see the inner area of the room. There is a large desk and a small Chinese man is standing behind the desk with both hands on the top. His chair is turning behind him. He has obviously stood up quite fast. I would say by the look on his face he can't believe that I'm in here and that his goon hasn't blown my head off, much less is holding the gun on him.

I walk up to the desk and plop my briefcase down, turn it toward him and open it. "You see this cash? I was ready to have as much fun in your establishment as I could. However, your guys here have left me feeling just a little unwelcome. So, what would you like to do to help me change my mind?" I turn the briefcase around to me but leave it open.

"I don't know who you are and I don't care how much money you want to throw around." He looks up at the big guy with the gun. "And as for you, you will pay for this dearly."

"Aw, I'm really sorry that you don't like me. I think you should sit back in your chair and think about your career. In fact as you think about this you will completely forget that I've even been here." I glance back at the big guy. "Both of you will forget."

Chang sits back in his chair. I wave my hand in front of his face and there is no reaction. I look around and spot a file cabinet that isn't locked. I slip the file folder out from the hidden compartment beneath the cash and put it in the cabinet. I close the briefcase and turn to go. "Gentlemen, it has been a pleasure. Hey, big guy, you will want to keep your gun on Chang until the police come in here and take over."

I slip out the door but stick a wad of paper in the buzzer so I can get back in easily if I need to. I casually walk over to Renee and whisper in her ear, "Five minutes before we need to exit." Aloud I ask, "Well, Darling, how have you been doing while I was gone?"

"Not too well, I'm only up by 2,000. I've done better at other places. Why don't we find a better location?" she answers, really hamming it up and sounding bored and spoiled. She pushes her chips to the dealer, "How about cashing me out?"

The dealer doesn't look happy but gives her $2,500. It's a good thing it's a high stakes table or we'd have to deal with the lady at the window.

Renee stands up just as all hell breaks loose. There is a tremendous loud thumping noise at the door where we came in. The raid has started early! Most of the bouncers head that way. Another starts shouting for everyone to head for the emergency exit that is located at the east wall instead of the south. There is pandemonium as chips and cash are flying all over and tables are being turned over. People are being knocked down, yelling and screaming all over the place.

I pull Renee back toward the office as people rush past. "There has to be a secret back door in the office. They wouldn't let the boss get captured in a raid." We head for the door and pull it open. I hear a loud crash behind us, probably the cops breaking in. I pull the paper out of the lock then slam the door just as a couple of shots ring out. We run past the big guy with the gun still holding it on Chang. I pull a curtain down behind Chang's desk to expose a door.

"Here's hoping our limo is waiting on the other side of that door and not a bunch of cops," says Renee.

I don't take time to answer; I just hit the crash bar on the steel door and fling it open. Sure enough the limo is idling just outside the door. I look quickly up and down the street and there are two cops guarding a door further to the east. There is a patty wagon backed up with its doors open ready to take anyone escaping from that direction.

We close the door and get in the limo. I wonder why the cops weren't covering this back door. As we drive off, Renee gasps, "Darryl, where did we come out?"

I look back and there isn't any door in the wall. It is solid brick.

"What's going on Darryl? How did that happen?" asks Renee.

I take a few seconds. A lot is running around in my brain. We have missing bodies, not to mention Joe and his shop. Now, we walk through a wall that had a door in it a few minutes ago. Is this due to our guardian angels or is The Voice taking care of us?

"I think we have someone watching out for us. We never could have pulled this off by ourselves." I relate to her what happened in the back room while she was gambling. "It's like I had total mind control over them. I can only attribute that to The Voice," I suggest.

"You know I'm pretty good at black jack but tonight in those few minutes, I couldn't lose," says Renee. "I'm not too sure, but I don't think angels help out gamblers."

We sit quietly for a few minutes as we navigate back to Queen Anne.

"What's this going to cost us?" asks Renee.

"What do you mean?"

"I just get the feeling that at some point your Voice is going to want a payback," she answers. "Have you ever known anyone who did favors and looked after others who didn't eventually want something out of it?"

"Well, sure, I don't think my parents were looking for a payback," I answer.

"No, I'm not talking about that kind of thing. The Voice is helping us do stuff that is illegal. He isn't doing this so we can feed orphans in Africa or other good deeds. Have you known anyone in our line of work that did favors like this who didn't want a cut of the action?" she asks.

"No, but The Voice isn't a person. He's a spirit of some kind. Doesn't that make his motives different?" I respond.

"Yeah, he's a spirit of some kind. I guess that bothers me because I can imagine a spirit would eventually want something that would be a whole lot more costly than material things." She seems quite glum about this.

"What, you think he's like the devil and wants our souls?" I suggest.

"Yeah, I guess that sums it up."

"You know that's all a bunch of crap." I shake my head. I can't believe she's considering that.

"Well, I guess we'll just have to wait and see," she says.

I'm not at all happy about her concerns. She's always been so level-headed and now she starts worrying about – I'm not sure exactly what she is worried about. Maybe it's superstition. All I know is that The Voice has been taking care of us and that's good enough for me.

We ride the rest of the way back to the house in silence. Once we get back, I go to check the late night news to see if there is anything about the raid on TV. Renee goes to bed without a word.

There is a brief mention on the news about police activity in the International District, but there aren't any details. I stay up to catch a re-run of the Star Trek re-run I missed last night. The Voice is right. The show was contrived to make us think that we couldn't handle having god-like powers. It's subtle how TV programs actually brainwash us into submission to society.

Chapter Fifteen

It's been over a month since the raid and we still haven't seen anything happening to Trickey. We've been holed up in this ratty house and we're both getting cabin fever. It's getting so bad that I had Felipe get some weights and one of the fancy new exercise machines. When I'm not pumping iron or running on the treadmill, I've been researching stocks for Rodney's portfolio.

OK, I haven't been doing so much research as I have been listening to The Voice as he instructs me to look for certain stocks in the paper. So far, with his advice I've almost doubled Rodney's fortune. If we keep this up, he'll become a billionaire in a little over two years. A lot of good that'll do if we can't get out of here and have some fun.

Renee has used the treadmill some also. But I'm getting concerned for her. She's been spending a lot of time reading spiritual books. One is a laugh, *Chariots of the Gods*, which tries to explain the existence of mankind by visits from aliens millions of years ago. Yeah, right, so where did the aliens come from? Not a very compelling answer to the age-old question.

She's also been reading books by Edgar Cayce and Mary Baker Eddy. It makes me feel freaky but The Voice hasn't protested in any way. I questioned him about it and he said she is just expanding her mind. Sooner or later, she will be able to accept him completely.

I'm interrupted from my musings when I hear a knock on the kitchen door. I venture into the kitchen and open the door for Felipe. He is definitely pleased, grinning ear to ear.

"So what's the news?" I ask.

"Oh you will like this," he answers. "Yesterday afternoon, the FBI and the Seattle Police Department made simultaneous raids on Trickey's office, Walston & Company, an insurance office on Capitol Hill, and several gambling locations. There were also several dirty cops arrested at the same time."

"Yes! So, we can finally get out of here and have a normal life," I celebrate.

"Uh, I also have bad news. He was released on bail just an hour ago," explains Felipe.

"Crap! This can't go on forever. Maybe your idea to eliminate him was the best idea," I grumble. It's amazing how fast elation can turn sour.

"So we're back to the same question, how do we eliminate him?" ask Felipe.

"Maybe we need to convince him it's time to leave town. After all, the feds are on to him and they have enough evidence to put him away for a long time. It isn't like there is a key witness against him that he can kill and destroy the case against him. That's for the movies. He knows it's only a matter of time before he's sent away," I think out loud.

"Just who do you think will be able to convince him?" asks Felipe.

"Maybe it's time for me to walk into the lion's den," I say. Is that me talking or is that The Voice? I'm not that brave.

"You gotta be kidding! He has a contract on you. How do you think you'll even be able to get past his first bodyguard?" Felipe obviously doesn't like the idea.

Renee enters the room. "Hi, Felipe. What's going on? I thought you guys were getting a bit loud out here."

Felipe explains what has happened, then points at me. "This guy now thinks he can just walk up to Trickey and convince him that it's in his best interest to take a long trip to South America."

"Yeah, that makes sense. After our foray into the gambling den I think he's getting a bit cocky," she says sarcastically.

I just scowl at her and Felipe shakes his head.

"Do you think he should really do it?" asks Felipe, not noticing the sarcasm.

"What? You are serious? I don't know, Darryl. I'm still freaked out about what happened in China town. If you do this, you'll have to do it on your own. I'm not coming with you," she says as she throws up her hands and turns away. "I don't even want to hear about the planning," she says as she goes to the bedroom.

"Fine!" I say loudly as the door closes. I turn back to Felipe. "It's probably best if she isn't involved anyway," I say. "She just hasn't been the same since then. I thought it was just being cooped up here all the time, but now I think there's more to it."

"Do you think it has to do with the books she's been reading?" asks Felipe. "I've noticed they are all on some weird spiritual paths. Maybe she's seeking some higher power or connection."

"You know about those books?" I ask.

"Si, Rosie tells me about the things Renee has asked her to pick up. Oh, that reminds me, here is another book she wanted. It's about Nostradamus," says Felipe.

"Who's that?" I ask

"He was a French apothecary and prophet. Apparently a lot of what he predicted has come true. Here's the weird thing; his mother's name was Renee. Maybe Renee feels some kind of bond to him and is looking for a spiritual channel," suggests Felipe.

"Apothecary – oh, that's weird," I say as I ponder whether or not she's trying to make some connection to Joe and The Voice and, yes, even to her own involvement being named Renee. "You might be right."

I continue, "Whatever; it doesn't matter right now. I need to set up a meeting with Trickey or better yet, maybe I should just pay him a surprise visit."

"Madre mia! You are loco. If you go there you will never come out alive."

"I don't know, think about this. I go to his office and manage to see him based on my persuasive skills. He is an arrogant SOB so he invites me in. I tell him that I now have complete control of all of Rodney's assets and Rodney is basically a pauper now. That takes all the heat off him so that Rodney doesn't have to be hidden," I explain part one.

"OK, for argument's sake, you aren't blown away and get to tell him this. He releases Rodney because killing him won't do any good," reasons

Felipe. "But how does this not just put you in that much more danger? Won't he just kill you on the spot for spite?"

"Yeah, I'm sure he will be tempted to do that. However, with Rodney's assets, I'll say I've put a contract out on him. If he drops the contract on me and leaves the country in the next twenty-four hours, I drop the contract on him. If he kills me or doesn't comply, then the contract is doubled. It will be enough to attract some pretty nasty assassins. What do you think about that?" I ask.

"If you come back alive, then it will work. But I don't give you much of a chance of that happening. You don't know these guys. They are killers and have been dealing with much tougher guys than you for years. Amigo, I say wait it out," replies Felipe.

"I don't have the patience for that," The Voice tells me to add, "and I have much bigger plans as soon as Trickey is out of the way. You, my friend, will be able to expand your operations." I wonder just what that means, but don't question him at this point. He has made it clear that the plan will work.

The comment about expanding Felipe's operation pushed a button.

"What do you know about my operation?" he asks with a scowl.

"Nothing. I only know you are well connected and are able to supply guys with guns for protection as well as other people in the Latino community. I'm not going to pretend that you have a licensed private detective agency so what you do isn't that much different from Trickey's operations. Your guys are acquainted with the gambling scene. You've probably been a minor player in the area and now, with proper funding you can do much better. Does that sound about right?" I ask.

Felipe laughs, "Si, you are right on all counts. If you survive your encounter, we can talk about your ideas. I will pray to Saint Nicolas for you to be successful."

"Santa Claus? What's that about?" I ask.

"Saint Nicolas is also known as the patron saint of thieves," explains Felipe.

"Huh, I would have thought you would pray to Jesus Malverde rather than a real saint," I say.

Felipe gets real serious, "What do you know of Jesus Malverde?"

"Uh, nothing, the name just came to my mind. Who is he?" The Voice gave me the name.

"It is better you did not know," replies Felipe.

"Ohhh – kay," I draw out and raise my hands enough to indicate I won't go there. "Let's get back to Trickey. Since you have eyes on him, I'll need to know when he's in his office."

"Si, you are correct, he is arrogant. He keeps a schedule which a boss shouldn't normally do. He does not fear any attacks. His driver always drops him off at 9:00 am and picks him up at 7:00 pm unless he has outside meetings, which are not often. He has various lunch meetings with important people during the week. They are usually at noon but can last until 2:00," relates Felipe.

"Perfect. Tomorrow at 9:00, I'll arrive at his building and make sure the limo drops me off just in front of his car. I'll be wearing that expensive suit you got and carrying a briefcase. I'll look just like any other businessman going to work or calling on a client. The limo will be an attention grabber." I think I have it all planned out, or I should say, The Voice assures me the plan will work.

"So how do you plan on getting to his office?" asks Felipe.

"That, my friend is going to depend on my charm." Translated, that means The Voice will work though me just as he did in the casino.

"OK, if that's the way you want it. However, we'll need to have an advance for the next month's operation because you aren't going to be coming back and we'll need to have the funeral expenses paid," says Felipe glumly.

"Nice try, Felipe, but you won't need it. Besides, you still have the diamond deposit."

"I was hoping we wouldn't have to cash them in this soon."

"Just have the limo here by 8:45 tomorrow," I answer a bit perturbed by his doom and gloom attitude.

Felipe leaves and I go to find Renee. I think it's time to talk about her reading material. I find her in the bedroom sitting on the bed snuggled under the comforter. The room is cold. Since this shack has only a gas heater in the little dining area between the living room and the bedroom, no heat gets in the room unless the door is open. I will be so glad when we can find a decent place to live. I have to stop and think about that for a second because this place is actually better than our one room apartment on the Ave.

"Hi Honey, what are you up to?" I ask as I walk in.

"Just reading," she answers curtly.

"Yeah, I can see that." I hand her the book Felipe brought on Nostradamus. "Felipe brought this book for you also."

She takes it from my hand without making eye contact.

"So what's going on? You don't seem to be yourself lately and you're reading all these books on spiritual stuff," I ask. I'm trying to show that I'm genuinely concerned without being prying.

"You mean beside the fact you're trying to get yourself killed? We've been cooped up in the dump for over a month, and your Voice has me worried that there is something beyond our senses that could possibly be very good but I'm wondering if it is really very bad," she blurts out.

I'm a bit stunned. Which one of these things is the main issue? There's only one way to find out and that's to take them one at a time. I take her hand, "Hey, you've seen what happened back at the casino. I'm positive that The Voice will take care of me when I visit Trickey," I assure her.

"What guarantee do you have that your Voice won't just laugh and let them kill you on the spot?" she asks. "I've been reading a lot of books about all sorts of spiritual beings and even going back all the way to the Greek gods; these guys have always been described as capricious. They have nothing but disdain for human beings. They toy with mortals and eventually dump them in the trash when they're done."

"Really?" I frown. "So you think that by trusting The Voice, I'm likely to get killed at some point? Wow, that just doesn't seem anywhere close to where he's been leading me. Just look at the stock tips. Without his input, I wouldn't have any idea of what to buy or sell. There hasn't been one transaction where we've lost money. He hasn't asked me to do anything that I can see would benefit him. Come to think of it, I don't know what would benefit him since he is the spirit of a long dead person," I finish.

Renee responds a little less agitated and grips my hand, "Yeah, I see that and it just doesn't make sense. He doesn't seem to fit in the pattern. I feel like I want some clear indication of his intentions."

"Well, I don't know what I could say or what he could do more than what he already has done to prove his intentions," I offer. "I'm really searching my mind to try to come up with something."

"Yeah, I can see the difficulty," ponders Renee. She pauses thoughtfully then continues, "However, I've also read some Christian authors who are quite convinced that any voice or spirit that doesn't acknowledge Jesus Christ would be demonic. Have you ever asked him what he thinks of Jesus?"

"Really? I hadn't thought of that. The next time he contacts me, I'll ask about that," I answer thoughtfully.

"You can't just ask him now?" asks Renee.

"Well I can ask but he doesn't always respond when I try to contact him. But he usually answers questions after he contacts me. Sometimes I have a question or thought and then he gives an answer later," I reply.

"So then, because we've talked about this, we can consider that he knows and will get back with an answer?" presses Renee.

"Yeah, I believe he will."

"Good. That might help, unless he comes up with something that is weird." She seems somewhat relieved. "You know, it will be really great to get out of here. I guess I know your visit to Trickey is something that you have to do, but it still scares me." She leans over and gives me a kiss on the cheek.

Chapter Sixteen

At 8:45 in the morning, the limo arrives and I leave the house and get in the back seat. Felipe is there.

"Morning, Felipe. Are you all ready for this?" I ask.

"From what I understand, there isn't anything for me to be ready to do except pray to the Virgin Mary that Trickey doesn't kill you," he answers sourly.

I smile, "I thought you were praying to St. Nicolas." I tease as if his prayers would do anything one way or the other.

"Si, him too, but I think that Mary has more pull in this kind of thing than does a saint." I still have to laugh inwardly at his superstitious religion. He continues, "If you do come out of this alive, I'll look forward to seeing what you have planned for the future."

"Ah, yes, the future. We can work on that as soon as Trickey is out of the picture and I'm not hiding in a hole on the side of Queen Anne," I say cheerfully. I'm feeling good today. This is going to be a fun adventure.

The limo heads down Gilman and makes a sharp turn onto 15th Ave West. It turns into Elliot Ave then we turn onto Denny Way passing the Pacific Science Center. Then we turn right onto 5th Ave and drive under the monorail, take a left on Blanchard, and make another left on 6th Ave. The driver pulls over to the right curb to wait for Trickey to arrive. It shouldn't be more than five minutes. The driver has been instructed to pull in front of Trickey's car as he drives up, and then block the curb at the entrance to the building.

Right on cue, our limo pulls out into traffic in front of Trickey's car. We continue the half block to the entrance to the Denny Building. I wait just long enough to make sure Trickey notices. I can see through the back window that his car has stopped and is waiting for us.

I step out of the limo and take a few steps toward the entrance, put my briefcase on the sidewalk and take out my wallet as if I'm looking for something. Trickey's car stops and one of his bodyguards gets out of the passenger side then opens the back door for Trickey. I pick up my briefcase and turn around to face him as he gets out of the car. I take two steps toward him and the bodyguard immediately steps between us. He pulls his left lapel back far enough for me to see his gun.

I wave my hand to my right, "You don't want to do anything rash, you want to step back and let me talk to Mr. Trickey." The guard steps aside as Trickey gawks in wonder.

I hear a hammer cock on a gun inside the car just before Trickey's second guard emerges from the vehicle. "You really need to put your gun away," I say to the second guard, "it would be way too messy to shoot someone out here on the street. You know, blood all over the place and then you'd have to explain to the cops why you shot me. No, not good at all."

"Get this guy away from me!" shouts Trickey but his guards don't move.

I extend my hand to him, "Hi, my name's Darryl Smith. We haven't met, but I'm pretty sure you know who I am. I certainly know that you're the one that's made my life miserable ever since I got Mr. McNairy's assets out of your control."

Trickey is not a happy camper. "You're a dead man," he says. He doesn't shake my hand but starts to get back into his car.

"No, we need to go to your office and discuss how we can resolve this little disagreement." I wave two fingers at the guard by the door and he steps in to block Trickey from getting back into his car.

Trickey turns around, his face has gone ashen and stammers, "Ho-ow, wha-at is going on?"

I shrug my shoulder and answer, "Beats me. I just want to talk to you in private and it seems that your guys are in agreement. Why don't we just peacefully go to your office, now."

"OK," he grunts through tight lips.

We walk in the front door and to the elevator lobby. We enter an elevator and one of the guards pushes the button for the 10th floor at the top of the building. We ride up in silence.

We get off the elevator and turn right to a hallway. Trickey's law firm is directly ahead of us. It has big glass doors with his name in gold on it. I start to walk toward the door when he speaks, "Let's use my private entrance down this hall."

"OK," I respond and we make another right and come to a door that simply says, "Private" on it. Guard number one uses a key to unlock the door and open it.

"After you," says Trickey.

So I enter the room and everything goes black as I feel a sharp pain to the back of my head.

When I wake up, my head is splitting and I can't move. Oh boy, I didn't see that one coming. I open my eyes but everything is a bit blurry. I can tell one thing and that I'm not in Trickey's office. I'm duct tapped to a chair. Not like the movies either with only a small piece of duct tape. I'm wrapped body, arms, legs, there is no way I can even wiggle my hands. The place smells damp and the walls are cement blocks. It could be the basement of the building or they may have moved me somewhere else.

"Oh, that hurts," I moan.

A goon sitting on a chair reading a newspaper looks up then gets up and leaves the room. A few minutes later, he comes back followed by Trickey.

"I don't know how you hypnotized my guards so fast, but you certainly aren't going to be able to do that again," he says. "I should just have you killed and feed you to the fishes. However, since you went through the trouble of wanting to talk to me, I'd like to hear what you have to say."

"Oh man, where do I start?" My head is not feeling like saying anything. "It's a good thing you didn't kill me because if I don't return from our meeting, a huge contract is going to be put on you. One so big even international assassins will be willing to come here for a chance at it."

"You don't scare me, punk. I know that you and your girl friend are nothing but small-time con artists. You wouldn't have the connections to do that," he sneers.

"Well, I have good enough connections to get into one of your Chinese gambling salons and plant the evidence that got you busted two days ago. How else do you think they made the connection between you and Clarence Sutherland?" I ask.

"You did that?" he asks rhetorically. "All the more reason to whack you."

"Let's get back to me putting a contract on you," I say. I need to get this back on getting rid of him instead of vice versa.

"Are you crazy, Kid? It doesn't work that way. No one puts out a hit on a boss or takes a hit on one. That would mean open warfare. This isn't that damn Godfather movie," Trickey laughs.

I hang my head. Why did The Voice convince me this was a good idea? The Voice tells me that it was the only way to get me face to face with Trickey. So now what am I supposed to do? He won't look me in the eye to give him the old evil eye trick and his goon is wise to it too.

"Go to hell, Trickey," I say as The Voice instructs me.

Trickey immediately clutches his chest and starts gasping for breath. He turns blue and falls face first on the concrete floor. The goon rushes to him and rolls him over. He feels for a pulse then turns to me with a drawn gun.

"What did you do?" he demands. "Undo it or I'll blow you away."

I have him, as I look into his eyes. "I just told him where to go and he went. Unless you want to join him, I suggest you untie me then call for a medic. One thing's for sure. You don't want them coming here and finding me tied up like this."

"Damn," he says as he takes out a knife and starts cutting the duct tape away. As soon as I'm free he starts toward the door.

"Just a minute." He stops at the door. "Make sure you tell the rest of your gang that if they try to fulfill Trickey's contract on me, the same thing will happen to them," I tell him firmly.

"Right! Just stay away from us," he yells as he exits the room.

I brush off some stands of the duct tape, step over Trickey's body and leave. I see the elevator to the left and get on. I was still in the same building but in the basement. I press the button for the first floor. As I walk down the stairs onto the sidewalk, I can hear a siren. My limo is parked across the street. The Medic One arrives and I take advantage of the stopped traffic and calmly walk across the street and get in the limo.

"Thank the saints that you are OK," says Felipe as I get in. "How did it go?"

"I don't think the saints had anything to do with it," I reply. "Let's head back home," I say to the limo driver. I don't want to reveal the details to Felipe.

"Mr. Trickey was quite accommodating. He and his two guards went to his office and we had a very calm, frank discussion about who would do what to whom if he didn't get out of town and never come back. He wasn't in agreement so I told him to go to hell. At that point, it looked like he had a heart attack," I explain very matter-of-factly.

"So the Medic One was for him," says Felipe. "What if they got there soon enough to revive him?"

"I'm quite sure he was dead and they won't be able to bring him back from where he went," I finish.

Felipe makes a sign of the cross.

"Now we need to get down to future business. I expect that you will hear from your contacts that the contract on me has expired, so to say," I laugh at that one. "Renee and I need to come out into the open and start managing Rodney's affairs better. So we need a really nice house. Do you have a real estate guy we can use?"

"Si, of course. Shall I have him come over this afternoon?" he asks.

"Yeah, that would be great. Renee needs to get out and what would be better than house hunting?"

"Then I'll need a ride to the stock brokerage right after noon so I can make some arrangement with them to streamline my trading." I'm running over things in my mind and thinking about what else needs to be taken care of soon.

"Darryl, you had some ideas about funding operations. It looks like you have survived, so what did you have in mind?" asks Felipe.

The voice had been filling me in on what we could do so I start to explain it to Felipe, "The way I see it, you might end up with the same problem as Trickey, taxes. Some of your income may not be achieved in a way that you can report, isn't that correct?"

"Si," he nods.

"What is one of the best ways to cover these funds and allow you to expand without suspicion?" I ask.

"The best way to do that is to have a legitimate business that deals primarily or substantially in cash. Unfortunately, they also require cash to start. Is that where you are headed?" replies Felipe.

"Yes, that's where I'm headed. If we are able to significantly increase Rodney's fortunes, and as long as I can keep up the track record, it will happen, then I propose that we invest some of that into restaurants that you will run. I don't know the details of exactly how we funnel the cash through them, but I suspect you know or will be able to find out." I wonder why The Voice doesn't give me any more details when he obviously knows more than I do.

"Si, it won't be hard to do. I feel very fortunate that we have been able to connect, and that you are still alive, I might add," says Felipe with a huge grin.

We arrive back at the shack and I step out of the limo. I watch as it drives off with Felipe. I turn to go into the house when Renee runs up the steps. She leaps up in the air and I catch her huge hug with her feet off the ground. It does my heart good to see her excited again.

"I'm so glad to see that you made it back. How did it go? Tell me all about it," she bubbles over.

We walk back down the steps and I relate the story to her. I don't leave out any details at the beginning because I want her to know that The Voice was in control all the time. Sure, it seems like I'm directing his power, but it is really him doing it all. I provide her with the same version that I told Felipe about the office. There isn't any need to alarm her with the details in the basement.

Renee is subdued when she hears that Trickey had a heart attack. "You told him to go to hell and he just died?"

"Yeah, that's pretty much the story. His goons were quite amenable to making sure we wouldn't be bothered again," I state confidently.

Renee tilts her head with a quizzical look and slowly says, "Sooo, you killed him?"

I pull back a bit at that question and answer, "No, how could I give a guy a heart attack?"

"Then your Voice guy killed him?" she presses on.

"I suppose you could say that, but how would we know it just wasn't his time and The Voice knew it? I mean I was threatening him with a contract. The stress may have been too much. He was rather angry," I try to reason. I'm quite sure The Voice did it but I need to soften this for her.

She bites her lip then agrees, "Yeah, you're right. But the timing is mighty suspicious." She takes a deep breath and sighs, "I guess the good news is that you weren't killed and I take it we are free to leave this dump?"

"Yes, my Dear, that's the best news. In fact, Felipe will have a real estate agent come over this afternoon so that you can go house shopping." I give her a little poke on the arm.

"Really? Wow, so where shall we look?" she asks.

"Uh, today it won't be we, but you. I really need to go the Merrill Lynch office so I can streamline the way I handle Rodney's account." I can see the disappointment on her face. "I'm sorry, but this is Friday and I don't want to wait until Monday. We'll have the weekend to look and plan. How's that?"

"OK, but Seattle is pretty big. What area would you like?" she asks.

"You know, I haven't thought much about it. Any place with you would be great." I think I did OK with that answer. She smiles and gives me a hug.

Chapter Seventeen

It's been six months since Trickey's death and it's a wonderfully beautiful Pacific Northwest autumn day. I have a small break to muse about what has occurred.

Renee liked the charm of the Capitol Hill area so we found a huge old mansion here that was completely remodeled and modernized. I was able to set up a corporation quickly to handle Rodney's affairs so that Renee and I are actually paid for taking care of him. We purchased the house through the corporation.

I work every day from the time the stock market opens until closing time, making trades as The Voice directs. In the last six months, Rodney's three million has grown to twenty-five million and that's after taking out eight million to invest in restaurants and cover other expenses.

I'm really excited doing all this. There is something about handling all the money, stocks, and properties that gives me a thrill. I'm reminded of Scrooge McDuck, Donald Duck's uncle from the comics I read as a kid. He would go into his vault and just sit in his money and enjoy it. I feel the same way.

Renee has been working on cleaning up the story we did on Rodney so he could avoid the draft. We were concerned that if anyone went to the records and believed that his condition was a result of an accident that occurred before he signed the Power of Attorney for us, we would be out of a job. After several medical exams and retrieving the false ones planted in the UW, we have a clear record and no fears. With Trickey's death we officially negated him as executor of Rodney's will and established us as executors.

Felipe has been very busy as well. With the infusion of cash and using the restaurants as well as Rodney's properties, we've been able to launder ten times as much cash as he did before. As a result, his organization has grown in strength, becoming the dominant force in underground gambling.

What is even more amazing is that he has been able to expand his drug trade to surrounding states and into Canada. Each month, we invest more of the stock earnings into another business that helps us in the overall goals that The Voice has laid out. We keep these details hidden from Renee as we've moved way past small-time cons. I'm afraid that she would object to the drugs.

I'm interrupted in my musing of the success of our operations by Renee coming into the upstairs office in the house.

"Wow, what a beautiful day," she exclaims as she stops in front of my desk and looks out the picture window overlooking Lake Washington.

I turn in my chair to look also. The autumn leaves on the far shore of the lake are brilliant, the sky is clear and blue and it all reflects in the calm water of the lake. "We don't get many days like this, do we?" I comment.

"No, but when they come they are well worth enjoying," she says whimsically.

"So what's up?" I ask. She doesn't often interrupt me during stock trading time.

She sighs then starts, "We need a vacation or something. I looked out the window and realized that we've been so busy, we haven't had much time together to just kick back and goof off. I kind of miss our laid back life B.R. Before Rodney."

"You miss not knowing if we'd have enough money for rent or groceries?" I ask, not wanting to go back to that at all.

"Don't get me wrong, the affluence is wonderful. But don't you think we ought to take advantage of it? Just how much has Rodney's company paid us since we set it up?" she says as she sits down on the leather couch by the desk.

I get up and sit down beside her. "I think our salaries have been somewhere around two hundred fifty thousand each, less taxes. Our expenses are all paid by the company, so what have you been doing with yours?"

"You know, I never thought I would say this, but I got tired buying clothes, especially if I don't have anywhere to wear them, like on a vacation – hint – hint." She slugs me on the arm.

"Ow," I protest, "I think I'm seeing a pattern here. Let me guess, you want me to take a break and go on some romantic trip, preferably to a warmer climate. Am I getting close?"

"Hmm, let me think about that. OK I'm done thinking. How about Hawaii for a couple of weeks? I've never been there," she says eagerly.

"Yeah," I hesitate. "I wonder how much it's changed. I got to see a bit of Oahu when I passed through in the Navy. I'll have to check to see if we have any big deals coming up, but we should be able to do that soon." I hedge because I really don't feel the need. Making money is just too much fun.

"Well don't wait too long or I may just decide to go by myself," she says as she gets up.

"Hey that might not be a bad idea. You could take Rosie and make it a girl's trip," I suggest.

"What?" she says as she turns around and scowls at me.

"What?" I answer and gesturing questioningly with my hands.

"You are such an idiot sometimes!" she blurts out as she stomps out the door.

I stew about that for a while but not too long. I only have an hour left before the market closes at 1:00 PM, then I can deal with Renee. The Voice gives me some instructions and I get on the phone and call in the trades. I sell some stock outright and buy some to cover short sales made in the morning. All told, I rake in a cool eight hundred thousand for the day's work. I'm going to have to give myself a raise.

The Voice comes down hard and reminds me that without him, I would still be trying to figure out how to pay rent. He is the one that deserves a raise and has just the investment in Felipe's organization that will do it.

Excuse me, but I thought your motives were primarily to be helping me. I seem to remember you saying something about getting on paths of enlightenment and things like that. Sure, I meditate every once in a while, but I haven't seen any guidance from you except on how to make more and more money and funnel it into Felipe's organization. Is this more for him or for me?

The Voice laughs, *You get your perks from this. You shouldn't question me too much. Just enjoy it while you can.*

What do you mean?

Darryl, Renee is right. You are an idiot if you haven't figured this out yet. You are a pawn and the bigger picture is expanding the drug trade. Haven't you seen the amount of money that's being laundered? Haven't you wondered where that money is coming from? Some is gambling, some is prostitution, but the bulk of it is from drug sales. I'm not concerned with money but want people to use drugs. Drugs destroy people and that's my payback.

I'm speechless, or should I say, thoughtless. The Voice is right. I should have put it all together before. I'm reminded that Renee had asked me to find out what The Voice thought of Jesus, so I ask. Who is Jesus Christ?

Again, The Voice laughs, *Oh yeah, you mean the dead carpenter who claimed to be God. I was around long before him and he's still kicking around here somewhere helping out a few people as he thinks best. But if you really want to know Jesus, you should get to know Jesus Malverde.*

He's the one that Felipe wouldn't tell me about. Who is he? I ask.

I am he, the patron saint of drug dealers. Why do you think I set you up with Felipe? It wasn't just to keep you from getting your butt blown off, he tells me.

If I'd know his goals, I don't think I would have listened to him. I'm ticked and feel betrayed.

So what's your decision, Darryl? Are you going to give up all this because you oppose the drug traffic or are you going to continue to cooperate? The Voice asks.

I think about that for a few seconds. Not long really, before I answer, No, I don't want to give this up.

A wise choice, Darryl, as you will figure out sooner or later, you are not indispensable. You don't have any time for vacations for a while either.

I don't like the sound of that but I don't say anything back to him. I'll just go with the flow. I head downstairs to give Renee the bad news. I find her in the living room with Rodney watching another of those damn Billy Graham shows. Fortunately this one has just ended.

They are both sitting on the couch with their heads bowed like they are praying. Oh, this doesn't look good at all.

"Excuse me, Renee, but we need to talk," I say as I enter the room.

She stands up and turns around. She's been crying.

Rodney stands up too and looks at me with a very befuddled expression.

The doorbell rings and I go to see who it is. The last thing I need right now is someone trying to sell magazines. It's Felipe so I open the door and he comes in. He takes a look at Renee with tears running down her face and Rodney standing there. Felipe seldom sees Rodney.

"What's going on?" he asks.

"That's what I was about to ask," I answer as I turn around and walk over to Renee. Felipe follows.

Renee starts to explain, "Darryl, it has all become clear to me. It finally makes sense. I was watching this last Billy Graham crusade telecast and I finally understood that Jesus Christ is God's Son. He died on the cross to take my sins upon himself. If he hadn't done that, I would go to hell to pay for all my sins. But he didn't die just for my sins; he died for yours, too. And yours, Felipe and yours, Rodney. All you need to do is admit your sins, ask for his forgiveness, turn from all this evil we are involved with, and he will save you. You will be with him forever in eternity. Oh, I'm so relieved that I've done it."

I'm speechless. All I can do is stare at her. I look at Felipe and he doesn't look like a happy camper either.

Then Rodney starts to talk, "These last seven months have been like a dream to me. But I heard every word that Billy Graham said on TV today. I, too, have turned to Jesus Christ as my Lord and Savior. As soon as I did, the fog went away and I can see the demon that has captured you, Darryl. Your only chance is to reject The Voice and turn to Jesus."

"You guys are crazy," I shout. "Just look at what we've accomplished. You have eight times the wealth you had before, Rodney. Why would you want to give that up?"

"I can't go back," says Renee. "I've decided to follow Jesus and no matter what happens, it is the better choice. If you don't want to make things right, then I'm leaving."

"I'll go one step further. If you don't make things right, then I'll go to the police," says Rodney.

I wave my hand from one to the other and give them the evil eye. "You don't want to do this. You will not leave or go to the cops," I command them.

"Your Voice has no power over us," says Renee, "we belong to Jesus now."

"Then to Jesus you will go," says Felipe as he quickly draws a gun and puts a bullet between Rodney's eyes and quickly shoots Renee.

Blood splatters all over the living room as both of them are flung backwards by the impact of the bullets.

"What the hell are you doing?" I yell as I turn toward Felipe.

He has the gun leveled at me and calmly says, "I can't have them telling the cops about this operation. Sorry, Amigo, but our partnership has just ended." He pulls the trigger.

I wake up to find myself in the most horrendous heat, even greater than I've ever experience. It is dark but I can feel fire all around me. I can smell the odor of burning flesh and hair. I bend over in agony; I scream out, "Make it stop!" There is no response.

Where is The Voice? I call but he doesn't answer. There is only silence.

Time seems to stand still but the pain and heat persist. I don't understand how I can possible survive, I want to die, I want to sleep, I just want it to stop but it continues. Somehow I continue to squirm and gnash my teeth but nothing helps.

How long I've been here, I don't know, but suddenly a bright light shines out of the darkness and illuminates a set of marble stairs. At the top of the stairs is a great white throne. The one sitting on the throne is brilliant, so intense that I can't look directly at him.

"Come up here!" commands a voice that thunders.

I discover that I have a body and can move, something that I believe was missing for who knows how long, even though I felt pain. I start up the stairs. Upon reaching the throne, I am compelled to fall on my knees before the magnificent person on the throne.

"Who are you?" I ask.

"I am Jesus, the Christ, whom you rejected and scorned in life," he answers.

"Oh, if I had only known, I would have believed in you!" I exclaim.

"Renee and Rodney both gave you a chance before you died and you chose the wages of sin over eternal life with me," he answers.

"Oh come on, I was a pretty good guy, I didn't kill anyone or –" I'm cut off before I can go further.

"These books contain all your deeds in your life. If there is but one transgression against me, then you will have earned eternal death unless in this other book, my book of life, your name is found because you have had faith in me to remove all your sins," he explains.

Oh, I'm in deep trouble. It doesn't take but a single page in my life to find my first sin at a very young age. He doesn't have to go on. He turns to the book of life and sadly shakes his head.

"I'm sorry; you had many chances but rejected them up to your final minute on earth. Depart from me into the eternal fires prepared for the devil and his angels. The one you called The Voice is there, but you will find no comfort from him, his torment is even worse than yours."

I am back in the horrendous heat, but now I know that it will never stop.

Epilogue

Renee and Rodney are immediately ushered into the presence of Jesus. "Welcome my good and faithful servants," says Jesus.

Renee falls at His feet and asks, "But how can you say that when I have been such a horrible person all my life? I only turned to you a few minutes ago."

"That is true, but I gave you the grace to have faith in me. I chose you before the earth was formed and it was your time to come to me when you did. Your testimony was true and was an added bonus."

Rodney also fell to his knees. "Lord, forgive me. I knew of you all my life but I never surrendered to your will. Yet here I am only because of your great love and compassion on me. Thank you so much."

"Raise, my children and enter into your rest," replies Jesus.

Felipe is haunted by Renee and Rodney's testimony for many years. Eventually he is arrested and convicted for his life of crime including the murder of Renee, Rodney, and Darryl. Because he cooperates with the investigation that takes down several drug rings, he is sentenced to life in prison rather than receiving the death penalty.

In prison, he comes to know Wilbur from Prisoners for Christ who comes to the maximum-security facility in Monroe, Washington. Over and over, he hears the message of forgiveness through Jesus Christ. At last he comes forward to find out if it is true that Jesus Christ will actually forgive even cold-blooded murder.

"Wilbur, you and friends have been coming here for years and I've been listening, but I can't believe that I can be forgiven for killing those people. Two of them had just turned their live over to Jesus and I shot them. How can I be sure he will forgive me?" asks Felipe.

Wilbur opens his Bible and says, "This is the New International Version of the Bible. It is easy to understand. I'll read from the book of

Romans, chapter 10, verses 9 though 11. 'If you confess with your mouth, "Jesus is Lord," and believe in your heart that God raised him from the dead, you will be saved. For it is with your heart that you believe and are justified, and it is with your mouth that you confess and are saved. As the Scripture says, "Anyone who trusts in him will never be put to shame."'"

"So Felipe, what does God say in his word" asks Wilbur.

"It says that anyone who trust in Jesus will not be put to shame," answers Felipe.

"That's right. How do you demonstrate your trust?

"Let me see again."

Wilbur shows the verses to Felipe.

"I need to say that Jesus is Lord, but I also need to believe God raised him from the dead. But I've believed these things all my life. I have been a Catholic all my life. I've know about Jesus all of my life," he responds.

"But have you ever trusted Jesus to save you?" asks Wilbur. "I would guess that if you were raised as Catholic, you always thought that you had to go to confession, never miss Mass, and do a lot of other things to be saved. In other words, your salvation depended not on what Jesus did to save you but on what you did. Isn't that true?"

"Si, that is true. So you are saying that all the things I did were worthless, that I can't earn my way to heaven?" asks Felipe.

"That's right. The Bible says that salvation is a free gift of God. In fact, if you think there is anything you can do to earn it, then it just proves that you haven't accepted that free gift. You are trying to pay for something that is available to you for free and your attempt to pay for it is an affront to God," explains Wilbur.

"So how do I get this gift? It seems like I must do something," says Felipe, still puzzled.

"Jesus Christ is the key to receiving this free gift of eternal life. Because we are sinners, there is nothing we can do to earn salvation, but Jesus, being God in the flesh, died on the cross to pay the penalty for our sins. Do you understand this?" asks Wilbur.

"Si, I have known that but this is the first time it has made sense," he agrees. "So what's still missing?"

Wilbur continues, "Part of confessing that Jesus is your Lord is trusting that He is the only one who can pay for your sins. However, you must also repent. Repenting is admitting that your sins are an affront to God, rebellion against Him and that you don't want to continue in them anymore. It is a change of attitude, admitting that God is right and that you are wrong. Do you understand this?"

"Si, again this now makes sense," replies Felipe.

"Good, then would you like to pray and ask Jesus to be your Lord and Savior?" asks Wilbur.

"Si, that would be wonderful, but I don't know how to pray like that."

"I'll help you; just repeat this prayer after me.

"Lord Jesus, I know I'm a sinner and can't save myself. Thank you for dying on the cross for my sins. Forgive me and take control of my life so that I can live for you."

Felipe repeats the prayer then Wilbur asks, "So Felipe, if you were to die tonight, where would you wake up?"

With a smile on his face, Felipe answers, "In heaven."

Then Wilbur explains to him that baptism is an outward sign of what has occurred in his heart. Felipe is eager to be baptized by emersion as a believing adult. They discuss arrangements to do this with the prison chaplain.

Felipe continues to serve his life sentence but also becomes a strong witness for Jesus Christ in the prison.

Other Books by Ray Ruppert

Novel

999 Years After Armageddon – The End of the Millennium, is a novel describing how Satan deceives the nations at the end of Jesus' 1000 year reign on earth.

Devotion

Reflections on First and Second Peter is a commentary on the epistles of Peter.

Education

Battling Satan with the Armor of God is a booklet on designed to help us understand Satan's abilities and the spiritual realm in which he operates so that we can use the armor of God to overcome his schemes and live a victorious Christian life.

Children's (Photographs by Ray Ruppert)

Cows for Kids Cow Fun and Facts is written by Malinda Mitchell. It is a fun filled learning experience about cattle.

Respect and Enjoy God's Creation is written by Malinda Mitchell. God's creation is all around us. Malinda Mitchell provides great tips for children to learn how to respect His creation.

These books are available in print and as e-books.

www.ingramcontent.com/pod-product-compliance
Lightning Source LLC
Chambersburg PA
CBHW071924220626
47052CB00002B/448